DOU

At first Jessica e
lighting was so st n
shadow. Across t was lifting
something out of the trunk of a white Trans Am. Something wrapped in a blanket. Jessica's heart was hammering wildly. She felt as if she was going to faint. It looked as though he were carrying a body. He was walking straight toward her, face lowered, the wrapped-up blanket in his arms. Jessica stared.

I'm just losing it, she told herself. *It's just some guy carrying something. Liz is right. I have been reading too many dumb detective stories.*

Just then the man stopped to hoist the load up, as if to get a better grip. Part of the blanket fell back as he shifted the weight, and Jessica felt her heart—almost literally—stand still. A woman's arm was clearly visible, hanging limply out from underneath the blanket.

At first Jessica thought she was going to scream. Her mouth dropped open, but no sound came out. She was standing absolutely frozen beside the Fiat when the man looked straight up at her, his eyes boring into hers. She knew she would never forget the expression on his face as long as she lived.

Bantam Books in the Sweet Valley High Series
Ask your bookseller for the books you have missed

#1 DOUBLE LOVE
#2 SECRETS
#3 PLAYING WITH FIRE
#4 POWER PLAY
#5 ALL NIGHT LONG
#6 DANGEROUS LOVE
#7 DEAR SISTER
#8 HEARTBREAKER
#9 RACING HEARTS
#10 WRONG KIND OF GIRL
#11 TOO GOOD TO BE TRUE
#12 WHEN LOVE DIES
#13 KIDNAPPED!
#14 DECEPTIONS
#15 PROMISES
#16 RAGS TO RICHES
#17 LOVE LETTERS
#18 HEAD OVER HEELS
#19 SHOWDOWN
#20 CRASH LANDING!
#21 RUNAWAY
#22 TOO MUCH IN LOVE
#23 SAY GOODBYE
#24 MEMORIES
#25 NOWHERE TO RUN
#26 HOSTAGE!
#27 LOVESTRUCK
#28 ALONE IN THE CROWD
#29 BITTER RIVALS
#30 JEALOUS LIES
#31 TAKING SIDES
#32 THE NEW JESSICA
#33 STARTING OVER
#34 FORBIDDEN LOVE
#35 OUT OF CONTROL
#36 LAST CHANCE
#37 RUMORS
#38 LEAVING HOME
#39 SECRET ADMIRER
#40 OUT OF CONTROL
#41 OUTCAST

Super Editions: PERFECT SUMMER
SPECIAL CHRISTMAS
SPRING BREAK
MALIBU SUMMER
WINTER CARNIVAL
SPRING FEVER

Super Thrillers: DOUBLE JEOPARDY

SWEET VALLEY HIGH
Super THRILLER

DOUBLE JEOPARDY

Written by
Kate William

Created by
FRANCINE PASCAL

BANTAM BOOKS
TORONTO • NEW YORK • LONDON • SYDNEY • AUCKLAND

RL 6, IL age 12 and up

DOUBLE JEOPARDY
A Bantam Book / December 1987

Conceived by Francine Pascal

Produced by Cloverdale Press, Inc.
133 Fifth Avenue, New York, NY 10003

Cover art by James Mathewuse

ISBN 0-553-26905-4

Published simultaneously in the United States and Canada

Bantam Books are published by Bantam Books, Inc. Its trademark, consisting of the words "Bantam Books" and the portrayal of a rooster, is Registered in U.S. Patent and Trademark Office and in other countries. Marca Registrada. Bantam Books, Inc., 666 Fifth Avenue, New York, New York 10103.

PRINTED IN THE UNITED STATES OF AMERICA

O 0 9 8 7 6 5 4 3 2 1

DOUBLE JEOPARDY

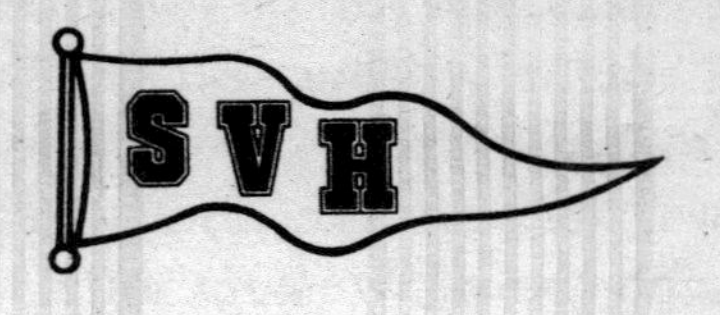

One

Jessica Wakefield's eyes sparkled with excitement as she burst into her twin sister's bedroom, ignoring the Do Not Disturb sign hanging from the doorknob. "Liz, you were right about our jobs at the *News!*" she exclaimed. "This is going to be the most wonderful summer of my entire life!"

Elizabeth couldn't help laughing at her sister's enthusiasm. For weeks Jessica had grumbled about the internships they had lined up at *The Sweet Valley News,* working as gofers and apprentice copywriters in the features department of the local paper. For Elizabeth the job was a dream come true. She had wanted to be a journalist for as long as she could remember, and her long hours working on *The Oracle*—the school paper at Sweet Valley High where she and Jessica were juniors—had taught her a great deal about writing. But Jessica thought writing was hard work. The whole point of a vacation was to have fun, and what fun could there possibly be in working long hours in an office?

"I don't suppose Seth Miller has anything to do with your change of heart," Elizabeth ventured with a smile.

Jessica grabbed a hairbrush from her twin's dresser and ran it through her silky, sun-streaked blond hair as she regarded her reflection in the mirror. "Well, I'm not going to pretend anyone *else* at the *News* is worth paying attention to," she said. "Lawrence Robb is as old as Dad. And everyone else there is either married or too nerdy to be believed." Her eyes twinkled. "Luckily, Seth Miller makes the whole thing worthwhile. I've got to hand it to you, Liz. When you roped me into this thing, I was kind of mad at you. But now . . ." She smiled dreamily as she set the hairbrush down.

Elizabeth laughed. Mad wasn't the word! Her twin had practically given her the silent treatment after their parents suggested that Jessica join her sister as an intern at the *News*. Jessica had had dozens of ideas about how to spend her summer, ranging from rafting in the Grand Canyon to hitchhiking around Europe to trying to get a job on a sitcom in Hollywood. Each plan was less practical than the last, and as June approached and nothing had been firmed up, Mr. and Mrs. Wakefield began to pressure Jessica to follow her twin's example and use her time productively.

Elizabeth recalled the battles that had taken place before Jessica finally agreed to work at the *News*. It was always during times like this that the Wakefield girls found themselves viewing the same situation in completely different ways. Although it was hard to imagine from a quick glance at the twins' identical appearance, they were opposites as far as their characters were concerned.

On the surface it was next to impossible to tell them apart. Sixteen years old, both girls were five-feet-six with model-slim, size-six figures. They had the same blond, shoulder-length hair and sparkling blue-green eyes. Each girl had a tiny dimple in her left cheek and wore a gold lavaliere necklace.

But anyone who knew the twins could testify to the fact that the similarity between them ended there. Steady, responsible, and forthright, Elizabeth believed in taking things slowly and following through to the end. She far preferred the company of a few close friends—such as Enid Rollins, her dearest confidante, or Jeffrey

French, her boyfriend—to the crowd her sister hung around with. She took her hobbies almost as seriously as her schoolwork, devoting hours to her writing. She was a natural leader and had won recognition from friends and peers as one of the most honest and dependable students at Sweet Valley High.

Sometimes Jessica couldn't believe she was even *related* to Elizabeth, let alone her twin. Jessica's philosophy was to have as much fun as possible. Adventure mattered more to her than almost anything else, and the one thing she absolutely couldn't tolerate was being bored. That meant that Jessica changed friends, hobbies, and fashions with lightning speed. One minute she wanted to be a professional dancer, the next she was obsessed with French cooking. It was so hard to keep up with her latest crushes and fads that the rest of the Wakefields—especially the twins' older brother, Steven—simply threw up their hands in despair.

Elizabeth had grown accustomed to watching out for her temperamental twin and doing her best to get her out of scrapes whenever she could. She couldn't help getting impatient with Jessica sometimes, but deep inside she loved her with all her heart and knew her twin would do anything for her. There was a special chemistry between them, and each could sense how the other was feeling without having to say a word. Right now, for example, Elizabeth knew that Jessica was feeling a host of conflicting emotions—gratitude to her twin for having organized the *News* internships; embarrassment at having put up such a fuss for the past few weeks about a summer office job; excitement about the vacation; but most of all, the heady rush of infatuation for Seth Miller, the young reporter from Washington, D.C.

"Admit it, Liz. Seth is a total doll," Jessica said passionately, hurling herself onto her sister's bed and looking up at her expectantly. "I don't see how you can *stand* working at the desk right next to his. I wouldn't be able to get a single thing done all day." She giggled. "In fact, I haven't been able to get anything done anyway. It's hard enough being on the other side of the newsroom from him." She hugged herself as she thought about the young reporter. Then, noticing Elizabeth's lack of response, a shadow crossed Jessica's face, and she abruptly sat up. "Liz, you're not in love with him, too, are you?" she shrieked.

Elizabeth patted her reassuringly on the arm. "Don't you remember Jeffrey?" she said dryly. "He's only been out of town for a week, Jess. And I have absolutely no intention of thinking about anyone else but him this vacation. Six weeks isn't *that* long. I think I can make it until he gets back!"

Jessica furrowed her brow. Her instinct had always been to discourage her sister from what seemed to her to be pointless faithfulness. Jessica found the idea of long-distance love completely boring. What was the good of having a boyfriend who took off for a job as a summer camp counselor in the San Francisco area, a whole day's drive away? Ordinarily she wouldn't have thought twice about giving her twin a lecture on the risks of getting tied down when she was only sixteen. But Jessica felt this was an extenuating circumstance. Seth Miller was too gorgeous, too obviously appealing in every way to encourage Elizabeth to be her competition. If her sister wasn't committed to Jeffrey, foolishly or otherwise, who could tell what disaster might ensue?

"Don't worry," Elizabeth assured her, her eyes twinkling as she guessed what her sister was thinking. "I know Seth's great, but he's all yours. That is, if you really think he'd be interested in someone our age. He seems a little old, don't you think?"

"He's only twenty-two," Jessica said promptly. "I just happen to have found his résumé in Mr. Robb's file cabinet."

"Jessica!" Elizabeth exclaimed. "That's a confidential document. You shouldn't have read it."

"I thought we were training to be reporters," Jessica objected. "We're supposed to learn how to investigate, right? And besides, the résumé was just sitting there—right in the file drawer. It wasn't locked up or anything."

Elizabeth shook her head. Why was it so hard to stay mad at her twin? Somehow Jessica could make *anything* sound reasonable! "Remember," Elizabeth reminded her sister, "we're not exactly training to be reporters. Mr. Robb made it very clear when we started working that basically we're consigned to run errands and do some basic editorial tasks until we prove ourselves." Secretly Elizabeth hoped that she could impress her boss enough to convince him to let her write a short article by the end of the vacation, but she knew it would take weeks of hard work.

But Jessica was obviously more interested in concentrating her efforts on Seth Miller. "Anyway, Seth isn't that much older than we are. He graduated from high school when he was sixteen," Jessica continued. "Sixteen! Can you believe it? He must be some kind of genius. And he whizzed through college winning every sort of award for writing imaginable, and then he got a master's degree in journalism, specializing in investigative reporting. And guess what else?"

Elizabeth groaned. "I can't," she said. "Jess, what did you do? Memorize this guy's file?"

"He writes mysteries in his free time," Jessica divulged breathlessly. "He's already published one, and he's working on the second. His pen name is Lester Ames. I've already been to the library twice trying to find his book, but someone's got it checked out." Jessica looked anxiously at her sister. "He's really more your type than mine," she confessed. "I mean, he's so serious about writing and everything. I wish—" She stared at Elizabeth as an idea occurred to her. "Liz, will you teach me everything you can about being a good writer? I want to impress Seth by writing the best piece possible and getting Mr. Robb to publish it!"

Elizabeth laughed at her sister's sudden eagerness. "You know I'd be glad to help you, but I don't know how easy it'll be to get Mr. Robb to publish one of your stories. He was careful not to promise us anything like that." She grinned. "Although at this point I doubt he has any idea you're so interested in writing. At the interview you made it pretty clear you wanted to be out of the office every night at five o'clock."

Jessica ignored this. "Imagine," she said

dreamily, "Seth might be the next Alfred Hitchcock—he'll make tons and tons of money and be really famous, and he'll write me into all his books and movies." She gave her twin an affectionate pat. "Don't worry, Liz. We'll let you work on our scripts or something."

"Thanks," Elizabeth said wryly. "But right now the only mystery I can see around here is how dinner is going to be ready on time when you haven't even started the spaghetti sauce. Mom and Dad are going to be home any minute."

Jessica was in another world and did not notice her sister's sarcasm. Just thinking about Seth Miller's curly black hair and gorgeous green eyes made her shiver. He had the most adorable little cleft in his chin and a deep dimple when he smiled, and he was just tall enough—and broad enough—to make his stylish clothes look fabulous. So far, it was true, he hadn't paid *that* much attention to her, Jessica thought. But she was confident she could change that.

In fact, Jessica had a good idea that before the week was out, Seth was going to be concentrating pretty hard on her. Just to make sure of it, she had a plan worked out. Because Seth Miller loved mysteries, she was going to be sure to supply him with enough stories to keep his head spinning. Jessica thought about her idea as she wandered downstairs toward the kitchen.

The mysteries she intended to fill Seth in on would be way too much for one man to solve alone, of course. This Sherlock Holmes was going to need a Watson, and Jessica had every intention of letting Seth know that she was more than willing to help him out!

That evening the Wakefields were relaxing on the deck behind their house, sipping herbal tea and enjoying the balmy, flower-scented California air. Ned Wakefield looked fondly at his twin daughters. "How's the newspaper business these days?" he asked, his eyes twinkling.

"Jessica's turning into a devoted reporter," Elizabeth said promptly, nudging her sister in the ribs. "Isn't that right, Jess?"

Jessica, absorbed in an anthology of detective stories, only grunted in response. But Steven, who had been idly tossing a softball in the air, never lost an opportunity to tease Jessica. "Don't tell me you're getting serious about something," he said with mock horror. At eighteen, Steven had his father's good looks—dark hair, dark eyes, and broad shoulders—and he shared an interest in his father's profession. He was home from college for the summer to work in his father's law firm.

Jessica shot him an injured look. "I don't get

any credit around this place," she complained. "Isn't it rotten the way they pick on me?" she appealed to her mother.

Mrs. Wakefield looked up from the design magazine she was flipping through. Slim and blue-eyed, the twins' mother was often mistaken for their older sister. She wore her smooth blond hair in a sleek pageboy cut and could fit into her daughters' clothes. She had a successful career as an interior designer.

"They're just teasing, dear," Mrs. Wakefield assured Jessica, her brow furrowed as if she were thinking about something else. "Steven, when did you say your friend Adam was moving in? I want to make sure to get the cot set up in your bedroom before he gets here."

"Adam? Who's Adam?" Jessica demanded.

"The ace reporter/mystery solver here didn't even know we're expecting a houseguest," Elizabeth said with a giggle. "Jess, where have you been? We've been talking about Adam for days!"

Jessica looked miffed. "Nobody tells me anything. Who *is* this guy? And why's he coming to stay with us? We barely have room as it is."

Elizabeth and Steven exchanged glances. "You don't have to share a bathroom with her," Elizabeth reminded her brother.

"Adam Maitland is one of my best friends from college," Steven told Jessica. "He's got a job at Wells and Wells, the criminal law firm downtown—you know, a summer internship like mine. His family's from South Dakota, and he can't afford to rent a place in Sweet Valley, so Mom and Dad said he could stay with us. It's only for the summer," he added.

Jessica looked as if she had just been delivered the death sentence. "Only for the summer!" she shrieked. "What do you mean, *only*?" Jessica had barely gotten used to the fact that her brother had moved back into the house for the summer. As it was, she'd have to move the clothes she had been storing in his closet back into her own—not to mention the boxes of records she had been keeping on his bed and the few little odds and ends that had managed to creep into his empty dresser drawers. "Mom!" Jessica moaned. "How could you guys *do* this to us? Don't you realize the bad effects that cramped living quarters can have on people? I was just reading about this study they did on mice, and—"

"Jessica," Mr. Wakefield said, flashing her a stern expression. "It's settled already. Adam Maitland is an exceptional young man. He's bright, hardworking, ambitious—and very dedicated to law. I was hoping he'd work for *our* firm but he's more intrigued by criminal law than by litigation. Anyway, his parents don't have a lot of money, and there's no way he can afford to rent a place this summer. Your mother and I were very proud of Steven for volunteering to share his room with Adam. We're all going to do everything we can to make him feel at home. Do you understand?"

Jessica sniffed. "I guess," she muttered.

Elizabeth leaned over and patted her on the hand. "It's OK, Jess," she said cheerfully. "He brought over some of his stuff a couple of nights ago when you were at Lila's house. He's incredibly cute."

Jessica didn't say anything. She just sat there fuming, wondering why her brother had to be so generous. The Wakefield house was charming, but it wasn't big. Her friend Lila Fowler, who was the only daughter of one of the richest men in the state, had a bedroom that was almost as big as the Wakefields' whole second floor!

Suddenly Jessica sat up straight, ignoring the detective anthology as it slid off her lap. Maybe it wouldn't be so bad having Adam move in with them. Here was a perfect opportunity to insure that Elizabeth didn't fall in love with Seth! After all, Jessica had been feeling more than a little guilty about her twin's romantic predicament. Hadn't she consciously slacked off on her campaign to lure Elizabeth away from her futile attachment to Jeffrey?

Adam Maitland might be the answer. Elizabeth thought he was cute, didn't she? It seemed half the battle was already won.

And they would certainly have plenty of opportunities to get to know each other. Especially since Adam was going to be living with them—right under the very same roof!

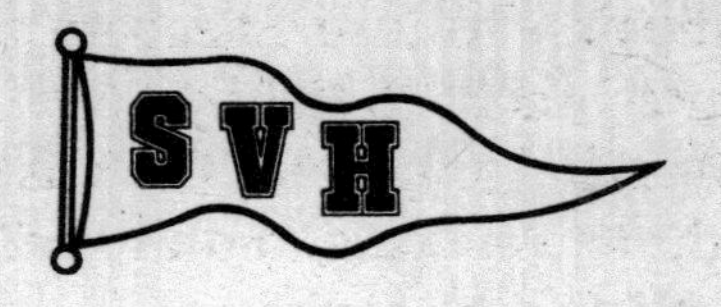

Two

"Listen to this!" Elizabeth exclaimed, looking up from the letter she had been reading. It was Saturday afternoon, and Elizabeth was enjoying the end of a long day at the beach with Jessica, Enid Rollins, and Lila Fowler. Enid, her best friend, knew exactly how much she treasured letters from Jeffrey. But Jessica and Lila exchanged impatient glances. Enid laughed appreciatively as Elizabeth read an anecdote from the letter. But Lila looked critical.

"Liz, don't you think Jeffrey's a little bit"—Lila frowned as she unscrewed the cap of her expensive French suntan oil—"*immature* for you?"

Enid giggled. She had just been complaining that morning that whenever Lila found fault with anyone, which was often, it was usually because she thought they were poor. But then, everyone was poor compared to Lila!

"Shh, let her read it," Enid said. "Go on, Liz."

> "Camp is starting to get to me already. Nothing like getting stuck with the nine-year-olds to make you wish you were back in school! Last night my bunk decided to treat me to their idea of fun. First they short-sheeted my bed. Then they put toothpaste in my slippers. Benjy, the biggest brat of all, put a frog in my trunk. I'm counting the minutes until I come home!"

Lila wrinkled her nose. "How juvenile," she said loftily, spreading suntan oil over her legs. "The camp *I* went to wasn't like that."

"That's because you went to finishing camp," Enid said. "I don't think they let you mess around with frogs in Switzerland."

"Liz," Jessica said, nudging Lila, "don't you think this vacation would be a good time for you and Jeffrey to test your relationship? You know, see how you two really feel about each other by going out with other people?"

Enid laughed. "Yeah. Jeffrey can go out with Benjy, for instance."

"I'm serious," Jessica said. "You two are so

dependent on each other, Liz. Don't you think a little new blood would liven things up? You know, someone older, more experienced . . ."

"What's Adam like?" Lila asked on cue. "From everything Jessica's said, he sounds terrific." She thought for a minute. "Poor, but terrific."

"He seems really nice," Elizabeth said. "I'm not sure how Jessica knows anything about him, since she hasn't even met him yet. But I guess that's beside the point, huh, Jess?"

Jessica looked hurt. "Just because I tried to give this guy the benefit of the doubt," she said sorrowfully. "I mean, here he is, moving into our house and taking up all kinds of space, and I'm being totally generous about the whole thing and trying to make the guy welcome. I can't believe my very own twin acts like I'm up to something just because I *suggest* she may have a tiny crush on him."

"Who said anything about my having a crush on him?" Elizabeth responded. "Jess, all I said was that he was cute." Clearly upset, she set her letter down. "You *know* I'm not interested in other guys. All I want this summer is to learn everything I can about journalism, maybe try to write a story good enough for Mr. Robb to publish. That's it! I miss Jeffrey like mad. Besides, I'm pretty sure Adam has a girlfriend. So cut the matchmaking, all right?"

Jessica sighed heavily. "Poor Adam," she moaned to Lila. "He's supposed to show up at our place tonight, and now I bet Liz won't even say *hello* to him or anything, she'll be so big on convincing me that she doesn't like him."

"Jessica," Elizabeth said, beginning to lose her patience, "I *promise* I'll be friendly to Adam—tonight, tomorrow night, as long as he's staying with us! Just don't make a big deal out of it. Because no matter what you say or do, I do *not* have a crush on this guy. And that, as far as I'm concerned, is *that*."

Jessica gave Lila a furtive smile. If Elizabeth thought the discussion was over, she had obviously forgotten how persistent her twin could be. Especially when it came down to something Jessica knew a little about. Like *love*.

"Tell us about your interest in law, Adam," Mrs. Wakefield said, refilling Adam's glass with minted iced tea. It was Saturday evening, and the Wakefields were out by the pool, barbecuing hamburgers and hot dogs and getting to know the newest member of their household. Jessica was watching Adam with fascination. Sure enough, he proved to be unusually good-looking. Tall, thin, with sandy-blond hair and elegant features, he seemed to be just Elizabeth's type—serious, intellectual, kind. He had a deep, quiet voice that demanded attention when he spoke. And to Jessica's delight, Elizabeth was listening more intently than anyone when Adam described his growing commitment to the study of law.

"My parents are farmers," Adam said. "Not exactly big-city folk, to put it mildly. But ever since I can remember, I've wanted to be a lawyer. Maybe I saw too many made-for-TV movies about lawyers when I was growing up. Who knows?" Everyone chuckled, and Adam seemed to relax a little. "That's how Steve and I met—in a class called Law and Society. I wish I were as naturally smart as your son, though. I have to work really hard to get good grades. I think I got a reputation for being a nerd this year since I spent most of my time studying."

"When you weren't with Laurie," Steve reminded him.

Adam blushed, and Jessica frowned. Laurie? The conversation was taking an unfortunate turn. It seemed to Jessica the best bet was to back things up and get him talking about something, anything, other than Laurie. "So tell us more about law," she interrupted, ignoring the look Elizabeth shot her. Jessica leaned forward intently. "It must be so *fascinating*, working at a law firm," Jessica continued. "My sister and I are working at a newspaper downtown. We'll all have to get together and compare notes."

Adam smiled. "That sounds like a good idea. Maybe we can even meet for lunch. The firm I'm working for is the new high-rise building—the Western Building. Is that close to where you two are?"

"Close?" Jessica exclaimed triumphantly. "We're in the Western Building, too—on the fifth floor."

"Wells and Wells is on the seventh floor," Adam said. "That's really a coincidence. We'll *definitely* have to meet for lunch."

"Tell us more about your family, Adam," Mrs. Wakefield urged. "I bet they'll miss having you at home."

"Well, they were a little disappointed at first," Adam admitted. "I think they missed me this year and were kind of hoping I'd come home for the summer. But they know how much I want to go to law school. Getting this job is a real break for me. If I do well and can get the partners to back me, I'll have a shot at a scholarship, which would pay for part of college and all of law school. My folks know how important that is. Besides. . . ." His voice trailed off, and he looked as if he were trying to decide whether or not to continue.

"Besides?" Mr. Wakefield prompted him.

"Well, my fi—my girlfriend, Laurie, is going to be at home this summer in San Mirando, about an hour from here. It would have been really hard for us to have been separated this summer. She's been going through some tough times, and I think she really needs my support right now. We're going to try to see each other on weekends, and just knowing I'm close by will really help."

Jessica sighed heavily. Great—just when she thought she had succeeded in getting the conversation back on track! Whoever this Laurie was, Jessica was sure she wasn't the kind of girlfriend Adam needed. All sorts of warning signals had shown her that. "Going through some tough times," "needing support,"—Laurie was obviously nothing but a drag! Adam was as bad as Elizabeth, getting involved in an intense emotional relationship at such a young age.

"Oh, dear," Mrs. Wakefield said uneasily. "I hope you'll feel like one of the family while you're here with us, Adam. If you should ever need advice about anything, or just want to talk things through . . ."

Adam seemed preoccupied. "You see," he said heavily, "Laurie's really all alone in the world. Her parents were killed in a plane crash in the Azores when she was a little kid. Her grandfather took custody of her but never had time for her—she was raised by servants. She's never really had a family at all. I'm all she's got."

Elizabeth looked sympathetically at him. "She must be incredibly grateful to have you around," she said softly.

Jessica held her head in her hands. Great! This was even worse than she had expected. If Adam felt sorry for this pathetic creature, there was no telling how difficult it might be to lure him away. But she was more convinced than ever that he needed a little fun in his life. This was going to be a bigger challenge than she had suspected.

"Who's taken care of her? Does she have any other relatives?" Mrs. Wakefield asked, concerned.

"Her grandfather is an oil tycoon named Tucker Hamilton. Have you heard of him? He's one of the richest men in the state," Adam said gloomily.

Jessica narrowed her eyes at him as she nibbled without appetite on a carrot stick. Adam was beginning to strike her as a little crazy. Why should a billionaire grandfather make him look ready to cry? She had a depressing sense that he might be the wrong candidate for a fling for her twin.

"Of course we've heard of Tucker Hamilton," Mr. Wakefield exclaimed. "If Laurie is *his* granddaughter, she must be a very rich young woman."

"Well, she would be—if it weren't for me. You see, her grandfather has some pretty harsh ideas about the world. When Laurie and I met last fall, he told her never to see me again. I'm a nobody as far as he's concerned. No family, no money. When Laurie refused, he threatened to cut her off without a cent. She couldn't care less about his money. She says she's had money all her life and no love and that she'd rather give up every penny and live with me than do what her grandfather wants her to do."

"Which is what?" Mr. Wakefield prompted gently.

"He wants her to marry the son of some man he does business with, a guy who's pretty unstable. Laurie went out with him a couple of times, to please her grandfather. She tried to tell Mr. Hamilton that this guy is unbalanced. But all Mr. Hamilton cares about is that he's rich, and to Laurie's grandfather marriage is like business—just another merger." Adam shook his head and said bitterly, "It's hard to believe that Laurie could even be related to him. She's the sweetest thing on earth. I know you'll all love her when you meet her."

I'll bet, Jessica thought. So much for the fun of watching a summer romance develop under the Wakefields' roof! Unless she could convince Adam to give up on this complicated mess with Laurie and concentrate his energies on her twin . . .

"One last thing," Adam said. "For Laurie's sake we've tried to keep her grandfather from finding out that we're still seeing each other. As long as she's dependent on him, we don't want Mr. Hamilton knowing about our romance. So we're doing everything we can to keep things secret."

"Well, he won't learn about it from us, Adam," Mrs. Wakefield said quietly. "Don't worry about that."

It looked as though it was going to take some hard work if she were really going to pull this one off! Jessica thought. Not that she didn't love a challenge. But clearly, if she was going to lure Adam away from this depressing, dead-end relationship, she was really going to have to make an effort.

"Jessica," Elizabeth said sharply, coming into the living room later that evening, "would you mind telling me what you think you're doing?"

Jessica was standing at the side window peering through her father's binoculars into the Bennets' yard next door. Her face was screwed up in concentration. "Shhh," she said. "I'm trying to see what Mr. Bennet is doing with that shovel."

"What shovel?" Elizabeth demanded. She snatched the binoculars out of her sister's hands and looked through them, but she saw nothing except a partially blocked view of Mr. Bennet's back as he bent over what seemed to be a small houseplant.

"He's been digging," Jessica said in a stage whisper. "Look—he's got dirt on his hands!"

"Jessica, he's transplanting something, you jerk," Elizabeth said, throwing the binoculars on the couch. "You can't just sit here and spy on people! It's an invasion of privacy."

Unperturbed, Jessica picked the binoculars up again. "You happen to be wrong," she said airily. "He is *not* transplanting anything. I know for a fact that he was digging in his garden for an entire hour tonight. And it had nothing to do with *plants*."

"I don't know what's getting into you," Elizabeth said. "You're reading too many of those detective novels, Jess. Mr. Bennet is about the last person in the world who would ever do anything worth spying on."

"That," Jessica said loftily, "just shows how much *you* know. It so happens that there are all kinds of strange things going on in this neighborhood. *You* might not think much of them, but I bet Seth Miller would."

"Aha!" Elizabeth cried. "So now we get to the bottom of it all! You're trying to come up with some kind of harebrained story to tell Seth Miller at work on Monday morning."

"Not harebrained," Jessica said hotly. "Can I help it if there's peculiar behavior going on all around me and no one else happens to show any interest in it?"

"Peculiar behavior," Elizabeth muttered. "The only peculiar behavior around this neighborhood is *yours*." With that retort she walked over to the television set and turned it on.

Jessica continued to watch Mr. Bennet through her binoculars. "I wouldn't be surprised if he's burying something," she said calmly. "Something like *evidence*."

"Yeah? Evidence of what?" Elizabeth demanded, throwing herself down on the couch and pushing the remote control to change channels.

"For instance," Jessica said thoughtfully, squinting at the kindly old man through the window, "did you happen to read that two thousand dollars was stolen from Federal Savings last week? The police don't know anything about the guy who did it, but just suppose—"

"Jessica," Elizabeth wailed, "I can't believe you're talking this way! Don't you realize you could be accused of libel? Poor old Mr. Bennet would no sooner rob a bank than—than—" Agitated, she broke off.

Jessica set the binoculars down and turned to face her sister. "That's OK, Liz. It's different for you—you want to be a features writer, not an investigative reporter. You're not interested in the sleuthing side of things."

"Jeez, from the sound of it you'll do a lot better writing fiction than writing for a newspaper!" Elizabeth exclaimed. "You'd better be careful, Jess. Don't start snooping around and accusing people of things. That's about the last thing a good reporter should do."

"Let's change the subject," Jessica said sweetly. "You're right about one thing, Liz. Adam Maitland is incredibly cute. A little too serious, maybe, but incredibly cute."

Elizabeth frowned. "What do you mean, a little too serious? I think he's fine just the way he is. You can't expect him to make fun of a situation like Laurie's." She sighed. "I really feel for him. Can you imagine how terrible it would be to really love someone whose family disapproved of you?"

Jessica didn't answer at once. "Well," she said at last, "I think Adam needs to forget about Laurie for a while. If he keeps seeing her, he's only going to break the one tie she has left in the world." She looked pointedly at her twin. "Maybe you can help him, Liz. If you spend some time with him, kind of give him some moral support . . ."

Elizabeth seemed unaware of her sister's motives. "You're right," she said thoughtfully, turning off the TV set. "I get the impression Adam is really lonely and frustrated right now. I think we all owe it to him to help as much as we can. If he's only going to be seeing Laurie on the weekends, he'll need a lot of companionship during the week. I'm going to do everything I can to make him feel at home here."

"You're great, Liz," Jessica said earnestly. "I can't believe how generous you are when it comes to situations like this." She picked up the binoculars again and smiled to herself.

With a little effort things could still go the way she wanted them to this summer. First on her list of priorities was coming up with some good solid evidence to present to Seth Miller on Monday morning.

And after that she could concentrate on helping Elizabeth and Adam to get to know each other better. Who could tell? Maybe the four of them would soon be double-dating!

Jessica narrowed her eyes as she stared out the window. The question was, what could she tell Seth she'd seen? So far nothing appeared out of the ordinary. Only Mr. Bennet puttering around with a spade, a hole in the garden . . . just about the size of the new shrubs she had spotted behind their shed. Not exactly the stuff thrillers were made of.

But then, it wouldn't take much imagination to make the whole thing seem much more exciting. And if there was one thing she had loads of, it was imagination. Especially when someone as wonderful as Seth Miller was at stake!

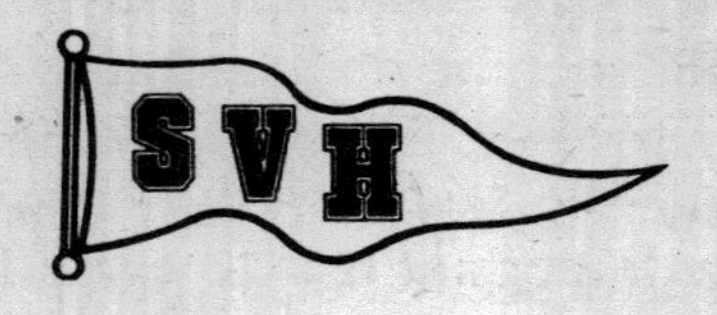

Three

Monday morning Jessica took ages getting dressed for work. She tried on three different outfits, none of them right, before settling on what seemed to her the most sophisticated, professional-looking clothing in her wardrobe—a straight, slim-cut black cotton skirt and a white cotton sweater. Newsprint colors, she thought happily, admiring the way the white sweater set off her tan. Seth couldn't help approve of how stylishly no-nonsense she looked. Next she agonized over her jewelry, switching back and forth between silver bangles on her wrist to long onyx drop earrings to a simple gold chain. By the time she came downstairs, Elizabeth was pacing up and down in the front hall.

"What's taking you so long?" she grumbled. "I promised Mr. Robb I'd get in early today so I could show him the story I did for *The Oracle* on the homeless."

Jessica smoothed back a stray lock of hair. "I'm ready," she said sweetly. "Liz, don't you realize how important it is to dress for success these days?"

Elizabeth rolled her eyes. "Yeah, especially when success means winning over Seth Miller."

Jessica ignored this slight. "Hey," she said, grabbing her sister's arm as the two walked out to the red Fiat they shared. "Look! It's Mr. Bennet. And he's digging stuff up in the garden again!"

"Jessica," Elizabeth said patiently as she opened the door on the driver's side, "it's summer. People like to work in their gardens in the summertime. Can't you find someone else to pick on instead of poor old Mr. Bennet?"

Jessica took a pair of sunglasses out of her purse. "I don't know, Liz," she said ominously, still staring at the neighbor's yard. "I think it's beginning to look pretty suspicious."

Elizabeth groaned as she started up the car. "I don't suppose this sudden interest of yours in Mr. Bennet's gardening has anything to do with the fact that Seth writes mysteries in his spare time?"

Jessica looked indignant. "Honestly, Liz. Can't I have any of my own interests? It just so happens that I've been noticing a lot of weird coincidences around this place lately. Just because *you* feel like ignoring them—"

"The only weird coincidence I've noticed," Elizabeth said, narrowing her eyes as she backed the Fiat down the driveway, "is that you seem to be wearing *my* gold chain for the second day in a row."

Jessica's eyes widened. "You're kidding," she said, all innocence. "Liz, how *thoughtless* of me. I could've sworn that I asked you if—"

"Never mind." Elizabeth laughed. Then she gave her sister a reproving look. "But the next time you start accusing poor Mr. Bennet of being mixed up in bank robberies, why don't you concentrate on whoever has been swiping things out of my room without asking lately?"

Jessica bit her lip and didn't answer. Clearly her twin couldn't see how important it was that someone keep an eye on Mr. Bennet. But she had a feeling Seth Miller would understand.

By the time the twins arrived at the Western Building, the municipal parking deck at its far end was almost filled. Elizabeth had to drive the Fiat up to the sixth floor of the deck before she found a spot, though usually they parked on the fifth floor, close to the newsroom entrance. "We're late," she said, looking upset.

Jessica leaped out of the car, frowning as she

looked around her. "I hate this kind of parking lot," she murmured. "It's really dark and spooky in here."

Elizabeth laughed. "You really *have* been reading too many thrillers," she said, giving her twin an impulsive hug. "Come on, let's get going before Mr. Robb gives us something *real* to worry about."

"Hey, there's Adam's car," Jessica said, pointing to the silver Volkswagen bug near the central bank of elevators. She gave her twin a significant sidelong look. "Maybe we can meet him for lunch today."

"I doubt it. Jess, I really want to impress Mr. Robb. At the rate we're going, we won't even be at our desks before nine-thirty. I'm going to work through lunch so I can make a few changes in my article before I show it to Mr. Robb."

Jessica sighed and cast a backward glance at the car. It really was too bad about Adam. Somehow, between getting Seth to pay attention to her and coming up with some viable neighborhood "mysteries," she was going to have to think of some way to get Adam and her sister together.

Jessica couldn't believe how cute Seth looked when he was hard at work. Sleeves rolled up and curly hair slightly disheveled, he looked as if he were straight out of a movie. He even had a pencil tucked behind one ear as he peered at the computer monitor on his desk.

"Seth," Jessica said when she was standing beside him, "can I get you a cup of coffee or something?"

Seth jumped. "What?" he said, clearly distracted. "Uh, no thanks, Jessica. I'm trying to wrap up this story on the fire at the Box Tree Café before noon."

Jessica picked up a pencil stub from his desk and stuck it behind her ear. She shifted her weight from one foot to the other and leaned over Seth's shoulder to read what he was writing on the screen.

Seth shifted uncomfortably and at last stopped typing. He turned to look at her inquisitively.

"You know," Jessica said, "I don't think that fire was an accident, Seth."

Seth stared at her. "What do you mean?"

"Well . . . maybe it's not that big a deal," Jessica murmured. "I probably don't have enough evidence yet to really be able to prove it was arson or anything."

Seth's eyebrows shot up. "Arson?" he demanded. "What are you talking about? What even gave you that idea? The reports I've looked at are pretty straightforward. Something caught fire in the kitchen." He frowned. "No one's said a *word* about arson."

"Oh . . . well, I'm sure your reports are right," Jessica said vaguely. "Anyway, you want to get the story done quickly." She glanced at her watch. "You probably don't have time to go over to the café and look around."

Seth pushed the Save command on his keyboard and turned around to face Jessica, his face serious. "Look, if you really have reason to believe there's something here I don't know about, let's go check it out. It's almost lunchtime, anyway. We can be back before Mr. Robb misses us."

Jessica's face lit up. "I knew you'd see things my way!" she exclaimed, rushing over to her desk to grab her purse.

She couldn't believe her luck—a chance to get Seth Miller out of the office so she could *really* get to know him. And who knew what they might find at the restaurant? Chances were that it really was nothing more than a kitchen fire. But after all, they were serious reporters. And didn't that mean they owed it to their reading public to make absolutely certain that no foul play had been involved?

"I can't believe you're really an author," Jessica gushed as they took the elevator together down to the fourth floor of the parking garage.

Seth drove a red Toyota Celica, Jessica's instantaneous vote for Car of the Year.

"Hop in," he said, very businesslike. Too businesslike for Jessica's liking. "Now, Jessica, what gives you the idea that there could be arson involved over at the café? Who tipped you off?"

Jessica's eyes widened. "A friend," she said, trying to sound as mysterious as possible. Wasn't that what they always said in movies? "I can't tell you any more, or I'd be getting my source in trouble," she added, thinking fast. "In fact, my source may be in trouble anyway. But, Seth," she added, cursing the bucket seats and wishing she could inch closer to him as they drove, "I want to know more about *you*. What brought you to the West Coast to write? Isn't Washington much more . . . you know, mys*ter*ious?"

Seth looked at her as though she had gone slightly crazy. "Not exactly," he said. "Too political for my taste. Anyway, I like the sunshine." He was about to say something more but then caught himself. "Let's forget the small talk for now, though. We've got a story to write, Jessica. If you can't tell me anything about your source, at least tell me what this person told you. What's the story?"

Jessica slipped her sunglasses out of her purse and put them on. She looked away from Seth as she spoke. "All I know is that they suspect arson," she said stubbornly. "I wish I could tell you more, Seth, but I just can't." She tried to sound steely, like the heroines in the new TV series she and Lila were hooked on. Men always seemed to flip over hard-core professional women who only cared about their jobs. Too bad journalism was so tedious, or she could be even more convincing, she thought. Mystery solving—or mystery *inventing*—was a whole lot more fun.

Ten minutes later Seth had pulled his Celica up in front of the Box Tree Café, a small restaurant downtown. The fire had been contained quickly, and no damage was visible from the outside. "Let's go in," Seth said, turning off the engine.

Jessica blanched. "Go in?" she repeated blankly.

"Yes," Seth said, looking at her peculiarly. "Why else did we drive down here? We're going to talk to the manager and see if he knows anything about the fire that he didn't reveal to me this morning on the phone."

Jessica fidgeted nervously. "Suppose—suppose my *source* gets in trouble," she said, clearing her throat.

"Jessica, what did you think we were going to do? We can't exactly learn anything just from standing out here and looking at the place," Seth said impatiently.

Jessica's face burned. "OK, OK," she said, jumping out of the car and following Seth into the restaurant. She was beginning to think this hadn't been such a good idea.

"Mr. Donaldson? I'm Seth Miller, from *The Sweet Valley News*," Seth was saying to a slim, distraught man who was talking to a man in a gray suit in the corner. "I called this morning and asked you a few questions. Do you remember?"

"Yes," Mr. Donaldson said. "I already told you exactly what happened. A skillet caught fire, some towels had been left too close, and they ignited. We've got thousands of dollars worth of damage," he added, staring sorrowfully at the charred kitchen

"This is my assistant on the story, Jessica Wakefield," Seth added. "We came down here because we have reason to suspect there may have been arson involved in the fire. Can you verify this?"

"Arson?" Mr. Donaldson gaped at him. "Are you kidding? I watched the whole thing. Unless you want to write a story about an omelet purposely causing a fire, I don't think you can do much from the arson angle." He and the other man both burst out laughing, and Jessica felt ridiculous.

"I guess my source was a little confused," she said, hurrying after Seth as he raced out of the café. His face was dark with anger.

"I'd say," he said shortly, opening the door on his side of the car.

"Seth, I'm so sorry," Jessica purred. "Promise you'll forgive me. It's just—" She paused, trying to think of the best way to defend herself. "It's just that I get so in*volved* in these things, I can't control my excitement." She looked meaningfully at him. "I really did think there'd been foul play, Seth. Please don't think I would have wasted your time if I didn't have a *very* good reason to believe there was more to the story than met the eye."

"Well," Seth said, relenting a little, "I guess you meant well. The thing is, Jessica, you have to be terribly careful in this business. If people think you're a jerk, you can get a bad reputation very quickly. Then when the *real* stories come up, no one wants to talk to you."

"I see," Jessica said quickly. Sensing he was thawing, she began to pump him for information about his former jobs. By the time they got back to the office, they were chatting easily—and Jessica couldn't help feeling that she had scored a major victory. Granted, things had seemed a little tense at the café for a few minutes. Next time she'd have to make sure she had a *real* story lined up.

But she was certain now that there *would* be more adventures with Seth. He liked her; she was sure of it. And whatever it took to keep him interested, however many mysteries she had to invent, Jessica was more than willing to do it!

"Lila, can't you stop listening to that thing? I want to go swimming," Jessica complained. She had been assigned the task of going to the library to do some research. Having finished early, she saw no reason to go back to the newspaper office. Instead, she had called Lila, and the two girls were now stretched out on striped towels at the beach, inspecting the surrounding shoreline for cute guys.

Lila wasn't very good company that afternoon. She was engrossed in her favorite soap opera, which she was watching on her Watchman and listening to through headphones.

"It's the very best part," Lila said, taking the headphones off to explain. "See, Vanessa—that's the redhead—has been telling everyone for *years* that she can't *stand* Timothy, the man with the curly hair and funny mouth. Now she's changing her mind and falling in love with him, all because she thinks he's in love with *her*. And the whole thing started because Janet, her cousin, planted a love letter from him in her purse." Lila put the headphones back on and peered down at the miniature TV screen.

Jessica was about to turn off the TV and drag Lila into the water when she suddenly had an idea. Wasn't it a basic fact of human psychology that people were much more likely to fall in love if they thought the other person loved *them*? It didn't take long to put two and two together—or in this case, one and one. Adam and Elizabeth.

"Lila," Jessica said thoughtfully, turning off the Watchman to get her friend's attention, "do you think that could work in real life? Let's say with Elizabeth, for example."

"What could work?" Lila asked blankly.

"You know," Jessica said. "Convincing her that someone was in love with her—let's just say by doing something like planting a letter from someone."

"Back up," Lila said. "A letter from whom?"

"Adam Maitland!" Jessica cried. "Lila, you've given me a wonderful idea. Liz just needs a little prompting, that's all. I mean, let's face it. She doesn't want to waste the whole summer sitting around missing Jeffrey. She needs a little fun in her life."

"And what does Adam Maitland have to do with fun?" Lila demanded.

Jessica gave her a pitying look. "You're really slow today," she complained. "Look, it's brilliant. It's absolutely perfect. All we need is a letter from Adam claiming he loves Liz more than anything in the world. That ought to get her started thinking about him in a more romantic way!" Suddenly she jumped to her feet.

"Where are you going?" Lila demanded, taking the headphones off and scrunching her face up at her friend. "I thought we were going to play water volleyball and try to get those two hunky blond guys to play with us."

"I've got to run," Jessica said breathlessly, stuffing all her things into her beach bag. "Now that I've thought of it, I can't waste another minute."

"Yeah," Lila said skeptically. "It's a great plan, Jess. As far as I can tell, there's only one thing missing. And that's a letter from Adam."

"Just leave that to me," Jessica said, grinning.

And without waiting for her friend's response, Jessica tore off across the beach, her eyes flashing with excitement. There was nothing she loved more than a plan. And a *plan* was exactly what she had just come up with!

"OK," Jessica said to herself, looking up from her sister's desk an hour later. She had come home to find the house deserted and had taken full advantage of her privacy. She had slaved over the letter, and she wanted to make sure it sounded like something Adam would write. Not that she could really fathom Adam saying any one of the wild things she had included, but then Elizabeth would never in a million years suspect her own twin of forging a love letter. The very last touch was the signature. After a good deal of deliberation, Jessica decided just to type Adam's name at the bottom. It would be too hard to try to imitate his handwriting, and far too risky.

The letter struck Jessica as perfect—farfetched, but perfect. All that was left now was for Elizabeth to find it. Humming cheerfully, Jessica slid the sealed envelope under her sister's pillow, then closed the bedroom door firmly behind her.

"I miss you, too," Elizabeth said huskily into the phone. It was so hard hanging up on Jeffrey! "When can you call again?"

"We're going on an overnight tomorrow," Jeffrey said. "If I survive, I'll call you as soon as I get back. But with twelve nine-year-olds and two days of hiking . . ."

"Take care," Elizabeth urged him. "I promise I'll write you first thing tomorrow."

"Good night," Jeffrey said. "I love you."

For a minute after she hung up the phone, Elizabeth sat still on her bed, filled with warmth and affection for Jeffrey. She smiled lovingly at the framed picture of him on her nightstand. He was so good-looking, with his blond hair and green eyes and that lopsided grin of his that made her stomach do little flipflops. It had been a long day, and Elizabeth was tired. She hated to break her reverie, but she knew she needed sleep. Automatically she turned the covers down on her bed, but to her surprise she felt something under her pillow. She withdrew an envelope and looked with interest at her own name typed on the front. She recognized the typeface—it was from her own beloved Olivetti, sitting right on the table she used as a desk. Someone must have come in, typed her a letter, and left it here. How strange.

"Dear Liz," the letter began.

> Please don't think I'm a terrible coward to write you instead of bringing this up in person. I guess I *am* a coward. If I weren't, I would have broken up with Laurie the minute I met you.

Elizabeth felt her face flush. She could barely believe it! Dropping her gaze to the bottom of the letter, she saw the familiar name, and her eyes widened with astonishment. Adam! Somewhat dazed, she continued reading.

> Liz, it's true. I'm in love with you. I know I haven't shown it, and the truth is, I won't be able to show it to you. Not yet. Not until I figure out what to do about Laurie. She's so vulnerable—I don't want to hurt her until I have to. So please be patient with me if I treat you like just another friend while I'm trying to get it all sorted out. You know you're not just another friend to me. I love you. I can't live without you. You're all I really want in this whole world, and if I can't figure out something soon, I may have to do something drastic.
>
> Love,
> Adam

Elizabeth's hand trembled as she read the letter again. But she had already made up her mind—there was no question about what she should do. Without a minute's hesitation she crossed the room and slipped the letter behind some books in her bookcase.

She wasn't going to say a word about the letter, not to anyone. Certainly not to Adam.

She was going to act just as if the whole thing hadn't happened.

Elizabeth couldn't fathom how Adam could have fallen in love with her. It seemed impossible, given everything she knew about his character. She was just going to have to hope that he had temporarily flipped, that the rough times with Laurie were beginning to get to him. But she knew one thing. She wasn't going to confront him about the letter. The most important thing for now was to show him that she wasn't, under any circumstances, going to do anything to encourage his behavior!

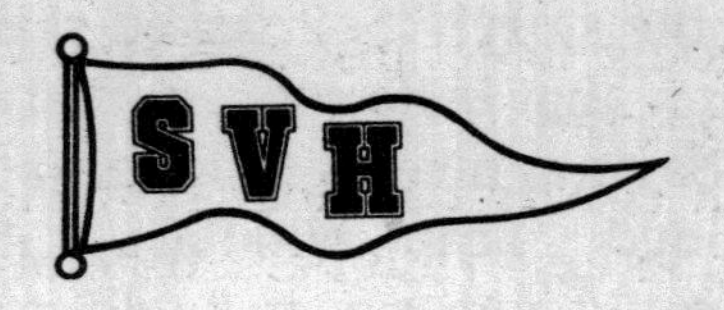

Four

"Seth!" Jessica cried, hurrying up to the young reporter's desk, her blond hair flying. "I've been looking for you everywhere."

Seth smiled in a noncommittal way. "Well, I've been right here," he said calmly. "You look as if you've just won the lottery," he added, noticing her flushed cheeks and sparkling eyes. "What's up?"

Jessica pulled up a chair and perched beside him, then glanced around anxiously to make sure that no one was within earshot. "I've got the story of the century for you," she said in a low voice. "I'm really serious this time, Seth. I know I kind of fouled up yesterday on that arson thing at the Box Tree Café. But this is an incredible scam. You've got to write it up and submit it to Robb!"

"What's the story?" Seth asked skeptically.

"You know that bank robbery that took place at Federal Savings a couple of weeks ago?"

Seth nodded. "Yeah. What about it?"

"What would you say if I told you I know who the robber was and where he's got the money buried?"

Seth stared at her. "Jessica," he said reprovingly, "this isn't fun and games, remember? This is a serious newspaper, and being a reporter is a serious job. Unless you've *really* got evidence . . ."

"Cross my heart and hope to die," Jessica pledged solemnly, her eyes wide. "This is for real, Seth. I promise."

Seth looked down at the story he had been working on about a postal workers' strike. The truth was, the story wasn't hanging together right. He had only a few hours to get something wonderful on Lawrence Robb's desk. It was a longshot, but if Jessica was telling the truth . . .

"You looked tired," Jessica said sympathetically. "Have you gotten any sleep lately?"

Seth pushed back his hair with one hand and shook his head. "I've been trying to do about seven million things at once," he admitted, sounding frazzled. "I've got to get the mystery I'm writing done in the next few weeks. On top of that, Robb's given me some killer deadlines here. And my mom's just had surgery, so I've been really worried about her."

"Let me help," Jessica begged, putting her hand on his arm and staring down at him with her most appealingly sympathetic expression.

Seth was obviously beginning to melt, despite himself. "I can't think what you could do," he muttered, looking helplessly at his computer screen.

"Just let me tell you everything I know about the robbery," Jessica pleaded. "That'll save you tons of time. You'll have a perfect story to give Robb in half an hour. I promise!"

Seth sighed heavily. "OK," he said at last. "I guess we could think about some kind of feature story. Now, Jessica, you know what you're promising me, right? You've got your facts absolutely right, and you're not the slightest bit fuzzy on any of them. Otherwise, we could both be facing the firing squad by lunchtime."

Jessica gulped. She was in deeper than she had planned already. What happened if Robb checked the facts and found out her story was much closer to fiction than journalism? She fidgeted uncertainly for a minute, but one look at Seth's expression made her mind up for her. If she wanted him, this was her chance. It was a big risk, but it seemed to her the only thing to do was to go ahead with her idea—and keep her fingers crossed. If she backed down now, admitting she was uncertain about the robbery, Seth would never show any interest in her.

"I know exactly what I'm promising," she murmured, brushing his fingers—as if accidentally—with her own. "I always do, Seth. I've got evidence, honestly. You've got to trust me."

Seth raised one eyebrow, then pushed the Clear button on his keyboard. The postal story disappeared, and blank screen faced them. "All right, then," Seth said, taking a deep breath. "Tell me everything you know about this thing, and let's see if you can put together a decent story before Robb starts demanding hard copies."

After a tentative beginning, Jessica regained her confidence. Within minutes she was pouring out a story that sounded impressively authentic, even to her. As she talked, Seth typed. She invented two witnesses and claimed that the police had suspected Mr. Bennet of embezzling small funds for years. By the time she reached the part about Mr. Bennet burying the money in his garden, she was so entranced by her own story that she almost forgot it was completely untrue.

"Whew," Seth said when she was done. "That's incredible, Jessica."

"Oh, well," Jessica said modestly. "I guess

you didn't take me seriously before, did you?" she asked huskily, inching closer to him.

Seth looked around them uneasily. "Uh . . . no. I mean, yes. I mean—"

"Never mind," Jessica purred. "The important thing is that you realize now how terribly serious I am." She dropped her hand onto his shoulder and let her fingers rest there for a minute. "I think you and I make a wonderful team," she continued.

Seth ignored her; he was typing in some changes in the story.

"Seth!" Lawrence Robb's voice boomed across the newsroom. He had a surly expression on his face as he walked toward Seth's desk. "Are you done with the story you promised me? I want to edit the thing and get it pasted up."

"Yes, sir," Seth said nervously. "Let me just print this out." Mr. Robb waited impatiently. "But it's not on the postal strike after all." He gave Jessica an encouraging smile. "With the help of my sidekick here, I've written a story I think readers will find much more interesting than just another analysis of the strike." Seth handed Mr. Robb the printout.

"Hmm," Mr. Robb said, looking at the story with an inscrutable expression. "You've got sources on this thing?"

Seth cleared his throat. "Uh, yes, sir," he said.

Lawrence Robb didn't look convinced. "I think I'll take a closer look at this in my office," he said thoughtfully, his eyes racing over the printed page. As Jessica watched him walk away, she had a sinking feeling in the pit of her stomach. Why had Seth made such a point of having changed his story? He had called so much attention to it that now Robb was bound to inspect it closely. And that was the last thing Jessica wanted to happen.

"Mr. Miller? Miss Wakefield? I'd like to see you both in my office," Mr. Robb said just as Jessica was opening the carton of yogurt she had brought with her from home for lunch.

Jessica shot Seth a quick glance. He looked pale now as well as exhausted. *Uh-oh,* she thought. *This is it.*

"I'm sure it's nothing important," she whispered to Seth as they followed the editor into his office at the end of the newsroom. "He probably just wants to go over a few grammatical points or something."

Seth looked miserable. "Why in God's name did I take your word on this thing?" he muttered. "Five years of journalism school, and all it takes is a pretty smile to make me forget the golden rule: Never take anyone's word for anything. Check your sources yourself."

Jessica bit her lip. Seth didn't exactly sound pleased. True, he had said she had a pretty smile, but he sure didn't look happy with her. "Maybe he's going to give us an award," she suggested hopefully. "This could be the best story to cross his desk in years."

"Yeah, keep dreaming." Seth groaned. "This is it. I finally wangled a great newspaper job, and now I'm going to get canned."

Jessica didn't think Seth was being all that supportive, but it didn't seem like the moment to argue with him. Mr. Robb closed the door to his office behind them and walked heavily over to his desk. He picked the story up as if it burned his fingers to touch it. "I want you both to know," he said heavily, "that in ten years as features editor I've never had to say what I'm about to say."

"Sir—" Seth cut in.

Mr. Robb put up his hand. "Let me finish. It's not simply that this story is irresponsible—no, *libelous*. It's not even that one single, tiny fact in it stood up when I tried to check them out. What pains me, Seth, is that I brought you out here with the hope of training you to become a real reporter. Now I find out that inventing mysteries isn't just a hobby for you—it's a full-time occupation."

Seth hung his head. His face was flaming red. "I can only say I'm sorry, sir. I behaved incredibly irresponsibly. I don't blame you for anything you've said."

Jessica took one long, quivering breath and promptly burst into tears. "I can't stand it," she sobbed. "It wasn't Seth's fault, Mr. Robb. I was the one who gave him the story. I—I *thought* I knew it was all true, but I guess—"

"You mean you took her word for it?" Mr. Robb demanded incredulously, turning back to Seth. "I'm not sure if that makes the whole thing better or worse."

"Please," Jessica said, trying to make her voice sound sincere and apologetic. "I'm the one who deserves to be yelled at, not Seth."

"You deserve more than yelling at," Mr. Robb said gruffly. Clearly the sight of her tears was beginning to get to him. "You deserve to lose your internship, right this minute. And you"—he turned back to Seth—"deserve nothing less than being fired!"

Jessica grabbed the edge of the desk. "You can't *fire* him," she pleaded.

"Jessica, shhh!" Seth hissed. "Don't you think you've caused enough trouble as it is?"

Stroking his chin thoughtfully, Mr. Robb looked from Seth to Jessica. "Well, you're both young and inexperienced. My guess is that this little fiasco has taught you both a serious lesson—one that some journalists never learn. Seth, I'll keep you on—on the condition that you swear this will never happen again."

"I swear it won't, sir," Seth said gratefully. "And I really appreciate a second chance."

"As for you," Mr. Robb said sternly to Jessica, "I don't see how I can justify keeping you on as an intern. We count on our interns to be exceptional—to help our young reporters, not to jeopardize their careers."

Jessica hung her head. "I wouldn't blame you if you kicked me out," she said. "I guess there's nothing I can do to prove how sorry I am, to prove that I realize how irresponsibly I behaved."

Mr. Robb looked at her thoughtfully. "You know," he said, half to himself, "I really can't see allowing you to continue in the features department. But I suppose you *could* help Sondra work on the data base we're trying to set up."

"Sondra?" Jessica whispered. Sondra Albert was a gruff, unfriendly woman in her early thirties. It seemed to Jessica that the only pleasure she got out of life came from the hours she spent sweating over the computer terminal. She was by far the last person in the newsroom Jessica would have chosen to work for, especially since she was known to be an incredible taskmaster.

"Yes," Mr. Robb said, smiling slightly. "That might work out quite nicely. Why don't you go clean out your desk and meet me over at the main computer in twenty minutes. I'm sure Sondra can find some special project to keep you busy for the next few weeks."

Jessica felt her eyes filling with tears. She didn't know which was worse—the humiliation of being kicked out of the features department or the grim prospect of working under Sondra's watchful eye. She wandered disconsolately behind Seth out of Mr. Robb's office, thinking that at the very least she had probably won his undying devotion for her heroic sacrifice.

"You don't have to thank me," she assured him once they were out of Mr. Robb's earshot. "I know I owed it to you, after getting some of my facts a little wrong."

"You're not kidding!" Seth said furiously. "Jessica, I ought to . . . I don't know *what* I ought to do to you. Do you realize how close you came to costing me my entire career? In fact," he fumed, "you probably *did* cost me my career. Robb will never take me seriously again, no matter what I do."

Jessica blinked. "You're . . . you mean you're not proud of the way I took all the blame in there?"

"Who else should've taken it? It was your fault, wasn't it?" Seth demanded.

Jessica stared. Seth didn't seem to be getting the picture. As far as she could tell, his position was exactly what it had been before the whole mess started. *She* was the one who had to go work for terrible Sondra in the smelly old computer room.

"I'm sure once you think about it you'll realize how unselfishly I behaved," she said self-righteously. "And you'll probably want to take me out to dinner or something. In which case—"

"You've got to be kidding," Seth snapped, stomping off and leaving her staring, stricken, after him.

Her plan had backfired. In fact, Jessica didn't really see how things could possibly be worse. She was going to have to explain the whole humiliating thing to Elizabeth and her parents. She was stuck with terrible Sondra and the computer for who knew how long. And Seth Miller hated her guts.

Oh, well, she thought sadly, dragging her feet as she headed over to her desk—her former desk—to gather up her belongings. There was one little ray of consolation in this whole mess. No matter how bad things seemed just then, they could only get better.

By ten that evening Jessica was completely bleary-eyed. She couldn't believe that Sondra really expected her to input all those figures into the computer. It was by far the most tedious work she had ever done, and the worst thing was that she'd only done half of what Sondra had asked her to complete. At that rate she'd be at the office until midnight! True, she had gotten a late start, since she'd had to spend so much time explaining to Elizabeth what had happened. And then her attempts to apologize to Seth had taken up a lot of time. But even so! Her head ached, her back ached, her eyes ached—and on top of all that, she was starving. She had practically worn a groove between the vending machines and the computer room, but now she was out of change, and she wanted real food anyway, not junk.

"This is ridiculous," she said to herself, rubbing her eyes. "I'm going to have to leave it and finish up tomorrow." She was the only person left in the office. Mr. Robb had gone home about half an hour before. Everyone else—

the ungrateful Seth included—had left ages ago. Even Liz had found a ride home and deserted her. There wasn't anyone left to appreciate her martyred labor, which was as good a reason for leaving as Jessica could imagine. It took several minutes to clean up the file she had been working on and to save her input, but at last she had all her things together. She turned out the lights in the computer room as she left.

Funny how different it felt walking into the garage this late at night, she thought. She was usually the last person to feel frightened in situations like this, but the parking deck of the Western Building had always seemed dark and threatening to her. There was a guard's booth near the elevator bank on each floor, but she noticed, without really making that big a deal out of it, that the booth at level five was empty. The fluorescent lights hummed a little as she walked to aisle J, where she had left the Fiat, her keys in her hand. She noticed Adam's unmistakable silver VW still parked in aisle L, where she had seen it that morning. So Adam was working late, too. For a second she thought about going to a pay phone and calling him. Maybe they could go out to dinner together. But it seemed like too much trouble, and at this point she really just wanted to get home.

She heard a crashing noise at the far end of

the garage and jumped. "Yow," she said aloud, rubbing her arms. She had goose bumps. This place really was creepy, she thought. She had just unlocked the front door of the Fiat when she heard something behind her. She felt a cold tingling go up and down her spine and in a terrified daze turned around.

At first Jessica couldn't believe her eyes. The lighting was so strange, and everything was in shadow. Across the garage a man—she could barely see him—was lifting something out of the trunk of a white Trans Am. Something wrapped in a blanket. The blanket was dark green, rolled up like . . . Jessica's heart was hammering wildly. She felt as if she was going to faint. It looked as though he was carrying a body. He was walking straight toward her, face lowered, the wrapped-up blanket in his arms. Jessica stared.

I'm just losing it, she told herself. *It's just some guy carrying something. Liz is right. I* have *been reading too many dumb detective stories.*

Just then the man stopped to hoist the load up, as if to get a better grip. Part of the green blanket fell back as he shifted the weight, and Jessica felt her heart—almost literally—stand still. A woman's arm was clearly visible, hanging limply out from underneath the blanket.

At first Jessica thought she was going to

scream. Her mouth dropped open, but no sound came out. She was standing absolutely frozen beside the Fiat when the man looked straight up at her, his eyes boring into hers. She knew she would never forget the expression on his face as long as she lived.

Barely even conscious of what she was doing, Jessica yanked open the Fiat's door and jammed the key into the ignition. She barely managed to pull the door closed as she shifted into reverse, the tires squealing on the concrete. She didn't take the time to watch where the man was going. All she could think of was getting out of that garage as fast as she could. She was trembling so violently she could barely control the car as she careened down the ramp to the fourth level, then the third, then the second, and finally—out into the open street.

The scene replayed itself over and over before her eyes: that horrible, intense look on the man's face; the white Trans Am behind him, with a rusted S shape scratched in the rear right side; and the limp body in his arms in that horrible green blanket, the pale arm dangling helplessly.

Tears of terror flooded Jessica's eyes, and she wanted to pull the Fiat over until she was calm enough to drive. But the sense that he might be following her was too strong.

It was almost impossible for her to absorb the full impact of what she had seen. But she was certain of one thing. The woman he was carrying was dead, and for all she knew, the man was the murderer.

She had seen him. Worse, he had seen *her*. She felt she had to get home as quickly as possible and find someone—anyone!—to protect her.

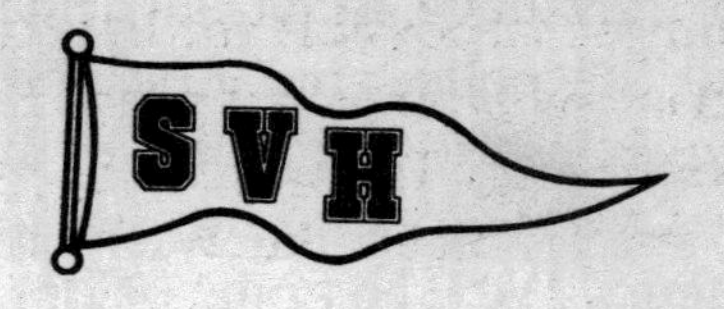

Five

The whole way home Jessica was convinced the man in the white Trans Am was trailing her. Her heart started pounding every time she looked in the rearview mirror. She kept thinking she saw a white gleam. Every time she turned the corner, she felt adrenaline coursing through her. Would the white car be there?

She was completely shaken by the time she got home and still trembling violently as she opened the front door. All she wanted was to fall into her parents' arms and beg them to reassure her that she was safe. But the house was completely empty. Only the front hallway light was on, the rest of the house was dark and quiet. Jessica drew a long, quavering breath and looked around anxiously. Where were they? Why now, the one time when she really needed them, did they have to be out? She knew she had to call the police, but first she wanted to tell someone close to her what she had seen.

"Jessica—we've gone to the late movie at the Valley Cinema. We'll be home before midnight," a note propped up on the kitchen table announced. Jessica shuddered. She couldn't believe how creepy her own house felt just then. Shadows from the houseplants in the living room flickered against the wall. The refrigerator hummed. A branch snapped. Then another. Jessica was shaking all over as she walked back out to the hallway. She could practically swear she heard footsteps upstairs. What if the man from the garage had managed to follow her home? She hadn't seen headlights behind her, but he could have done it, he could have sneaked in, he could— Something in the living room fell over with a crash, and Jessica screamed, clapping her hand over her mouth. It took her several seconds to realize it was only Prince Albert, the Wakefields' frisky dog, who had just woken from his late-evening nap and hurled himself headlong into the magazine rack in the living room, knocking it over.

"God, I'm really a mess," Jessica muttered, patting Prince Albert on the head with her trembling hand. She still couldn't believe what she had seen in the garage. Someone had been murdered, and for all she knew, she was the only witness. She felt faint as she remembered the outline of the body beneath the green blanket. "I'm going to crack up if I have to stay here alone for the next hour," she told Prince Albert, who cocked his head at her curiously. "I've got to call someone."

Prince Albert barked encouragingly, and Jessica, still shaken and pale, walked back to the kitchen and dialed Lila Fowler's number. She felt overwhelming disappointment when the answering machine came on after the second ring. Next she tried Amy Sutton, one of her best friends, but again had no luck. Each disappointment seemed to make her fear more vivid. The thought of calling the police and recounting what she had seen only intensified her terror. She needed someone to be with her before she could recount her story. But who? It was at least a full minute before she thought of Seth. Of course. He would help her! She couldn't help feeling somewhat better as she dialed Seth's home phone number, which by a stroke of luck she had managed to sneak out of the private list of employee phone numbers in Mr. Robb's office earlier that week.

"Seth?" she said the minute he picked up the phone. "It's Jessica. Jessica Wakefield. Seth, I'm in terrible trouble. Can you come over here right away?"

"What . . . what time is it?" he asked sleepily. "Isn't it the middle of the night?"

Jessica was taken aback. It hadn't occurred to her that Seth might be in bed already. "It's not even eleven," she said. "Seth, I'm really serious. I need you to come over here. I'm all alone in the house, and I'm scared to death. Seth, I saw something so awful tonight. . . ."

"Right," Seth said sarcastically. "I suppose you saw one of your neighbors planting petunias or something. Or maybe you saw someone trying to set your street on fire with his barbecue."

"Seth!" Jessica cried. "I'm not kidding this time. I mean, I wasn't kidding the other times, either," she amended hastily. "But *this* time—"

"This time you're extra-serious," Seth mocked her. "Listen, Jessica, I don't think I have to explain to you that I had a rough day today. I came home with a headache so bad I thought I was going to have to call my doctor. Instead I took two aspirins and got into bed. And I actually managed, against all odds, to fall asleep. And *then* you know what happened?"

"What?" Jessica asked softly. She didn't care how grumpy Seth sounded. As long as he stayed on the phone with her, so she didn't have to listen to all those terrifying sounds around her, she was satisfied.

"Then *you* called." Seth groaned. "And now I'm smack back in the middle of the same old rotten day I was hoping I could forget forever."

"Seth, I need your help. I saw something tonight—" Her voice broke off. "Seth, I saw something tonight so terrible that I—" She couldn't even manage to finish the sentence without a choked sob. "I think I need to call the police. But I'm too scared. Seth, *please* come over and help me. Just come over and stay with me until my parents get home."

Seth seemed to sense that the urgency in her voice was legitimate this time. "You're not playing tricks on me again, are you?" he said doubtfully. "You really sound bad."

Jessica began to cry in earnest. It took all her self-control to steady her voice enough to give him directions to her house. "Please hurry," she begged. "I'm all alone here, and I'm terrified."

Seth sounded fully awake by now. "Give me your address then. I'll be over right away," he promised. "Just try to stay calm until I get there. Then you can tell me exactly what you saw."

Staying calm proved to be much easier said than done. Jessica was practically a basket case by the time Seth's Celica pulled up fifteen minutes later. She was so grateful to see him, she almost wept; when she saw how attentively he listed to her story, she completely forgave him for having been so harsh with her earlier that day.

"Hmm," he said when she had finished. He got to his feet and reached for his car keys.

"Where are you going?" Jessica shrieked. "You're not just going to leave me, are you?"

Seth frowned. "Nope. I want you to come with me. I want you to show me exactly where you saw that white car."

Jessica paled. The last thing on earth she wanted was to get anywhere near the Western garage. "Forget it," she said. "I'm never going anywhere near that garage again."

"Jess, we have to go! If he's still there, we can get a more accurate look at him. We can get his license plate numbers to give the cops. We absolutely *have* to."

Jessica shuddered. "You don't understand. If you'd seen what I saw . . . that hand sticking out . . . and Seth, the look on that guy's face! He stared right *at* me," she added. "I know he's going to come after me. He's going to want to kill me now because I'm a witness!"

"Jessica, you're hysterical," Seth admonished her. "I know how frightened you are, but I'll be there to protect you. Come on," he pleaded.

"We really have to hurry. If there's any chance of finding him . . ."

Jessica fought back tears. She didn't want Seth to think she was a baby, but the thought of going back to the garage made her panic. The memory of that cool, damp smell . . . the long shadow of the man as he came closer . . . and that arm. She struggled for composure. "I think we should go straight to the police," she said.

"Let's just go to the garage first. Then we'll go to the station," Seth said. He put his arm around her to steady her as they left the house, but Jessica was still trembling badly. He helped her into his car. Her fear seemed to mount as they got closer and closer to the now-dark parking garage.

Level five of the parking lot was mostly deserted when they pulled up to the guard's booth. The fluorescent lights had been dimmed, and the half-light made everything look unreal—even the blue columns had a ghostly look to them. The white Trans Am was nowhere to be seen, but even so, Jessica had goose bumps. Every time she heard the slightest noise, she jumped, convinced the white car would turn in and trap them. She kept the door locked on her side of the Celica and cowered in the seat as they drove around the lot. When they turned the corner,

Jessica noticed that Adam's car was still parked in aisle L. But her mind barely registered that fact. She was so eager to get out of the garage that she could barely think straight. Her stomach felt fluttery as Seth slowed down at the guard booth. If only he would step on the gas and go! She wanted to get to the police station. A car roared away behind them, and she was almost dizzy with fear. But it proved to be a light blue Mercedes. For the moment, at least, they were safe.

"Excuse me," Seth said pleasantly to the short, affable-looking guard who opened the door of his booth and stepped out when he saw them pull up. "We wanted to ask you a few questions. My friend saw something peculiar happen here tonight—over an hour ago. Did you leave your booth at all tonight, or have you been here all the time?"

"I've been here all the time," the guard said defensively. "Nothing peculiar could have happened without my knowing about it."

Seth glanced at Jessica and frowned. "Jessica, was he on duty here when you came out of the office?"

Jessica shook her head. "No one was here," she said. She remembered, with a sinking feeling in her stomach, that the guard booth had been empty. That was just before she had seen the man carrying the body. "Seth," she said in a low, urgent voice, "can't we get going?" She looked nervously over her shoulder.

"Look, miss," the guard said, beginning to get angry, "I can *prove* that I've been here all night. If you're going to start accusing me of not being on the job . . ."

Jessica looked at him, confused. *Had* he been there? She was almost positive the booth had been empty. But she had been tired and in a hurry, and perhaps her eyes had been playing tricks on her. "I'm really tired," she whispered to Seth. "Can we get out of here?"

Seth looked anxiously at her. "Just a minute," he said. "I really want to ask him a few more questions."

Jessica fidgeted nervously and kept turning to check behind them. She was absolutely convinced that at any second the white Trans Am would reappear.

Seth turned back to the guard, his expression concerned. "Sir, we have reason to believe that a serious incident may have occurred here tonight. Can you tell us anything about the security in this garage? How easy would it be for you to miss seeing something out of the ordinary?"

The guard frowned. "This is a public parking garage, and we don't require passes, if that's what you mean. But there are guards on each level, and we're all very careful." He looked thoughtfully at Seth. "I *did* step outside to make a phone call for about ten minutes this evening. Other than that, I've been here the whole time."

"What time was that?" Seth demanded.

He scratched his head. "I honestly don't remember. But it might have been about an hour ago—that seems about right."

"So he could've dumped the body and driven off before the guard came back," Seth said to Jessica.

Jessica felt cold all over. She wanted to get out of the garage more than anything in the world. "Please," she said in a low voice, "let's go back to my house and call the police from there, Seth. I have to get out of here."

Seth nodded. He thanked the guard, then explained that they would be contacting the police and there might be more questions for him later. And with that they drove off, leaving the dark garage behind them.

"Please come with me," Jessica begged Seth. They were parked in front of the Wakefields' house, and even though the bright lights indicated that the family was back, Jessica couldn't bear the thought of walking alone from the car to the house. Her teeth were chattering, and her heart was still pounding.

"I'll walk you to the door, but I think you should talk this over with your parents alone," Seth said. He patted her arm sympathetically. "I know you're upset, Jessica. But it isn't going to help matters to get so excited. Just try to stay calm. The most sensible thing is to tell your parents exactly what you saw. Then you and your dad can go over to the police department and file a report."

Jessica drew a long, shuddering breath. "You do believe me, don't you?" she asked, her tone pleading. "Seth, I couldn't stand it if you thought I was making all this up."

Seth was quiet for a minute. "Well, this isn't the best day to ask me about believing you," he said finally. "But look, one thing is obvious, and that's the fact that you're really upset. I think the best thing for you right now is to be with your parents and to get some rest. You're as white as a ghost."

Jessica bit her lip. Seth thought she was lying. He thought this was just like the other stories she had told him! "Thanks for coming over tonight," she said dully. She got out of the car and slammed the door before he could come with her up the walk.

She couldn't believe how frightened she was,

just rushing from the car to the house. In her haste to leave with Seth earlier, she discovered that she had forgotten her key. She banged on the door with all her might, but it seemed like ages before her mother opened it. "Why, Jess," her mother began, looking at her daughter with surprise and concern.

Jessica promptly burst into tears and threw her arms around her mother. "Mom," she sobbed. "I'm so glad you're home!"

"Why, honey, we were beginning to get concerned about you," Mrs. Wakefield said, stroking her hair as she held her close. "What's wrong? Where have you been?"

Jessica wiped the tears from her cheeks. "Where's Daddy?" she cried. "I need to talk to you both. Something awful has happened."

"What is it, Jess?" Elizabeth demanded, rushing over to her twin and giving her a hug. "Did something happen to you?"

"You look pale, honey," Mrs. Wakefield said. "Let's go into the living room and sit down. Your dad and Steve are there."

Mr. Wakefield jumped up as Mrs. Wakefield helped Jessica into the room. "Jessica, are you all right?" he asked, his voice full of concern.

"Just give me a second, and I'll explain everything," Jessica said grimly, sitting down on the couch. Her mother sat down beside her, and her father sat down again in his chair.

Jessica's tone was serious enough to alert the whole family that something was genuinely wrong. "I worked late tonight at the paper," she said once she had their undivided attention. "We can go into *why* later," she added, for her twin's benefit. "Anyway, I stayed till about ten. By the time I left, the garage was almost completely deserted. The guard's booth was empty. I was just getting near the Fiat when I saw—" Her voice broke off, and she covered her face with her hands.

"Honey," Mrs. Wakefield said, tightening her arm around her. "What did you see? Tell us!"

"This man." Jessica shuddered as the scene flashed back to her. "Oh, God, it was awful. It was absolutely awful," she said in a shaken voice.

"Is that it? What else happened, Jess?" Steven prodded.

"Steven," Mr. Wakefield said reprovingly, "your sister's upset. Why don't you give her a chance to tell her story her own way?"

Jessica was too distressed to register this exchange. "He had this—this *thing* in his arms. It was a blanket—I mean, it was wrapped in a blanket. It was—" She broke off again.

"Honey, try to tell us exactly what you saw,"

Mrs. Wakefield said gently. "I know you're upset, but we're having a hard time following you."

"It was a body," Jessica blurted out. "This guy was lifting it out of the trunk of his car and carrying it somewhere. I could sort of make out the shape of it through the blanket . . . and I could tell it was a girl. Or a woman, maybe. Anyway, she wasn't very big—not much bigger than *me*. And then, the most horrible part, I could see an arm—" Her voice broke off with a sob, and she began to shudder violently. "He saw me," she added in a whisper. "He looked right at me. I know he's going to try to come after me!"

"Did you call the guard? Or notify the police?" Mr. Wakefield asked, frowning.

Jessica shook her head vehemently. "I just wanted to get out of there as fast as possible. I jumped in the Fiat and was back on the street in about ten seconds. I was too scared to do anything. . . ." She began to shudder again. "I know I should've gone straight to the police. And I was too scared to get his license plate number, too. But I did notice something important about his car."

"What's that?" Steven asked, his expression suggesting that he couldn't yet decide how seriously to take all of this.

"There was this kind of rusted-out mark on the side. Sort of like an S. And he was driving a white Trans Am," Jessica said triumphantly.

"Jessica," Elizabeth said mildly, "I hate to bring this up right now, but haven't you been"—she fumbled for the right word—"kind of *excitable* lately? I mean, haven't you been seeing an awful lot of things that the rest of us just haven't noticed?"

Jessica's face burned. "If you're referring to that incident at work, Liz, why don't you just come right out and accuse me of being a liar?"

Elizabeth looked indignant. "I didn't mean that. Jess, don't be so defensive! I was only pointing out that it just seems like you've been a little jumpy lately." She looked significantly at her parents. "Like imagining poor old Mr. Bennet was a bank robber, for instance."

"Jessica!" Mr. Wakefield exclaimed. "What on earth—"

"Look, if you want to tattle on me, why don't you just drag out the whole sordid story?" Jessica said harshly to her sister. "But do me a favor and just let me finish first. What I saw tonight was real. Somebody was killed, Liz. Killed! And I can't see what good it's going to do just to sit around and talk about it. Daddy," she added, turning to him with a desperate expression in her blue-green eyes, "I want to call the police."

"Now, let's just slow down here," Mr. Wakefield said, putting up his hand. Years of training in the courtroom had taught him that a few well-timed questions could save an awful lot of work farther down the road. "Jessica, I want you to calm down for a minute. Try to clear your mind and think *very* carefully before you speak. And then I want you to try to tell us, again, *exactly* what you saw tonight."

Jessica repeated her story. This time she described her phone call to Seth when she got back to the house and found it empty, and their trip back to the garage. "I know Seth doesn't believe me," she concluded. "I guess I don't blame him. I made up a couple of stupid stories to impress him, and now he thinks I'm completely feeble."

Elizabeth frowned. "So the guard at the booth claimed that he was there the whole time?" She was beginning to look less skeptical now, and more concerned.

Jessica nodded. "That's what he said at first. Later he admitted he was gone for about ten minutes, making a phone call. Anyway, wherever he was, he certainly didn't want to admit he'd left the booth. He could probably lose his job if he admitted that he had taken a break.

But it hardly helps if he makes me look like a liar!"

No one said anything for a minute. "I know what you're thinking," Jessica said quickly. "You're all wondering whether or not I've gone completely off the deep end."

"Oh, sweetheart, we are not!" Mrs. Wakefield exclaimed, leaning over to give her a hug.

"Look, I suggest we all get a good night's sleep," Steven said, yawning and getting to his feet. "It's after midnight, and we've all got to be up early. Why don't we just sleep on the whole thing and call the police first thing tomorrow morning?"

Jessica's eyes filled with indignant tears. "Steven, this is an emergency!" she cried. "Don't you understand that?"

She turned to her father again. "We've got to call them *now,* Daddy. How can anyone even *think* about sleeping when this guy could be out on the loose somewhere?"

Steven rolled his eyes. "Emergency or no emergency, I'm going to bed," he announced, oblivious to the desperate expression on his sister's face.

"Hey," Elizabeth said suddenly, staring at her brother, "is Adam upstairs already? He never said good night to any of us. And I don't think I heard him come in."

Steven blinked. "That's right," he said slowly.

"I wonder—" He left the room and came back a few moments later. "His car isn't here," he said, worried. "I can't believe he's still at the office. Even a workaholic like Adam doesn't stay past midnight!"

"His car was still at the garage when I left," Jessica said. "In fact, it was still there when Seth and I went back to check things out. Maybe he *did* stay late. He's awfully serious about doing a good job."

"Yes, but not this late," Mrs. Wakefield said. "This is crazy! Ned, do you think he's all right?"

Mr. Wakefield rocked back and forth on his feet, the way he sometimes did when he was really worried. "It doesn't seem like Adam not to call. Jessica, what time did you say that you and Seth went back to the garage?"

Jessica was just opening her mouth to answer him when the phone rang.

"I'll get it!" everyone said at once, jumping up.

"That must be Adam," Steven said.

"*I'll* get it," Mr. Wakefield said firmly, walking into the kitchen and picking up the receiver. The whole family followed him. "Hello?" Mr. Wakefield said.

A long silence followed, and everyone watched anxiously as Mr. Wakefield's eyes widened in astonishment. "What?" he cried. "You *what*?"

Jessica and Elizabeth exchanged horrified glances as they saw their father grow increasingly upset. He mentioned Jessica being in the garage. By the time he had hung up, they were beside themselves.

"Tell us what's going on, Ned," Mrs. Wakefield said nervously.

"That," Mr. Wakefield said, sitting down on a kitchen chair and putting his head in his hands, "was the police. It seems Adam has been detained. They're keeping him in custody until they can call a grand jury to make an indictment." His expression was grim. "You're going to hear it sooner or later, so I might as well tell you straight out. Adam has been charged with first-degree murder."

"What?" Steven cried. "What are you *talking* about?" The color drained from his face. "Adam Maitland wouldn't hurt a flea! Who on earth are they saying he *murdered*?"

A chill ran down Jessica's spine as she saw the expression on her father's face.

"Laurie Hamilton," he said heavily. "Apparently Adam claims he found her body in the trunk of his car at eleven-thirty tonight. She'd been strangled. Adam called the police at once, who found a length of rope—which seems to have been the murder weapon—in his glove compartment. They've charged him and are assembling a grand jury to indict him sometime tomorrow. They want Jessica to come to the station immediately to file a report on what she saw in the garage."

Steven began pacing wildly. "How can they possibly suspect Adam? Do they really think he'd call them if he'd been the one who killed her?" he hollered. "How could they! Adam loved that girl more than anything in the world! Are they really stupid enough to think he'd kill her?"

No one said a word. *Laurie Hamilton,* Jessica thought, closing her eyes. A shudder ran through her. All she could think of was the outline of that body underneath the dark green blanket.

Laurie had been murdered. The question was, who was the man Jessica had seen carrying her dead body? And why in the world had he put her body in the trunk of Adam Maitland's car?

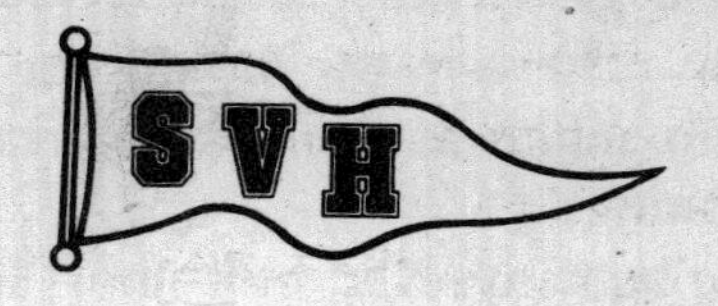

Six

"OK," Sergeant Jack Wilson said, blowing on the cup of coffee he had just extracted from the police-office vending machine. "Tell me again what time you saw this white Trans Am."

"I left the office a little after ten. It must've been about ten-ten. Maybe ten-fifteen," Jessica said. She was sitting next to her father, on the other side of Sergeant Wilson's desk. It was one in the morning, and both she and her father were exhausted. It felt as if days had elapsed since they had received Sergeant Wilson's phone call.

"Ten-fifteen," Sergeant Wilson said slowly, writing on the pad of paper in front of him. "Now you know we've already questioned a Mr. George De Luca, the guard who works the six P.M. to two A.M. shift in the booth on the fifth floor of the parking garage. Mr. De Luca claims he left the booth for just a few minutes to make a phone call and saw absolutely nothing."

"Maybe he's involved in it, too!" Jessica cried. "Because he lied to me when I went back to the garage and asked him about it. At first he said he hadn't left the booth at all," she added stubbornly.

The sergeant glanced at her, wrote something down, and put the tips of his fingers together before he spoke. "I'm afraid we really don't have much to go on here," he said quietly. "No one else in the parking garage around that time saw a white Trans Am."

"What about Adam? How is he?" Mr. Wakefield asked anxiously. "Can we see him?"

"He's talking to his lawyer now. If you come back tomorrow afternoon, you can see him then," the sergeant said. "Adam has had his rights read to him. A young associate from Wells and Wells, the firm where he's been an intern, has agreed to represent him. He's called his parents, too, and they intend to fly out here as soon as they can. Meanwhile, this case is our first order of business. This is an emergency, and we're putting absolutely everything else on hold. A grand jury has been called for the morning. If Adam is indicted, we'll keep him here, under close surveillance, until a trial date has been set. You'll be allowed to visit with him as long as an officer is present." He frowned. "I should mention that Adam is inconsolable. He was incoherent when we picked him up at the garage." He cleared his throat and looked uncomfortable. "We had to call a doctor to sedate him in order to—uh—to remove the body."

Jessica stared helplessly at her father. He had to be able to do something to get Adam out of this mess. Thank heavens he was a lawyer—at least he would know what to do! But to her dismay, Mr. Wakefield looked confused and worried.

"What's bail been set at?" he asked.

"Half a million," Sergeant Wilson said. He frowned. "The truth is, sir, that it doesn't look very good right now. The victim, Miss Hamilton, was obviously strangled. As I told you earlier, what looks to have been the murder weapon, a length of rope, was found wrapped in rags in the back of Adam Maitland's glove compartment."

"But anyone could have put it there," Jessica objected. She ignored her father's silencing look. "That doesn't seem like real evidence to me," she continued.

Sergeant Wilson raised his eyebrows at her. "Young lady," he said sternly, "it's the only evidence we have right now."

Jessica started to object again, and Sergeant Wilson raised his hand to silence her. "Adam Maitland had been dating Laurie Hamilton for six months," he continued. "They were secretly engaged last month. Laurie was due to come into an enormous amount of money two weeks from today—a trust fund that matured on her eighteenth birthday. Apparently Adam knew all about this trust fund. He also was pushing the idea of a secret marriage. We have reason to suspect Miss Hamilton may have begun to plead with him to delay."

Mr. Wakefield ran his hand wearily over his face. "What else?" he asked quietly.

"Adam Maitland has run up quite a few debts," Sergeant Wilson said gravely, toying with his pencil. "Debts to the tune of a couple of grand. He bought a used car, for example. Spent quite a bit on textbooks. Bought some clothing. It all adds up. It looks like he borrowed five thousand dollars from an aunt back home who suddenly lost her philanthropic streak and has started demanding that he repay. Apparently he's been under quite a bit of pressure to start paying some of the money back."

"I don't get it," Jessica said. "What does any of this have to do with Laurie getting killed? I *saw* that guy carrying her body. And it wasn't Adam! It was a blond guy."

"We need to be very careful," Sergeant Wilson said slowly. "I appreciate how upset you are, Miss Wakefield. Even though it's late, what we'd like to do now is to sit down and ask you for as detailed a description of this man, and his car, as you can give us. We're going to have you talk to our artist, who will draw a composite based on your description. What you've told us is extremely important, and we're obviously going to do everything we can to trace down this man. But I can't make any false promises, either. It's true Adam was the one who notified us. But the body was found in his trunk, and the rope in his car. We can't dismiss the fact that right now he's our chief suspect."

"What about Adam? When can he come home?" she demanded.

"We can't raise half a million dollars in bail, honey," Mr. Wakefield said, sighing. "I'll call his parents in the morning. But we know *they* can't afford it, either."

"You mean he has to stay in jail?" Jessica shrieked, horrified.

"He isn't in jail," the sergeant explained. "He's in custody, which is different. Believe me, Jessica, we're doing everything we possibly can. We know, at least partly, what he's going through, and we're really trying to help him." He shook his head. "Nothing like this has ever happened in Sweet Valley. I've been with this department for twenty-five years, and we've never had a murder here before. Frankly, we're all frightened. And none of us knows exactly how to proceed." He got up to shake Jessica's hand. "You've been very brave, Jessica. And we're going to have to ask you to keep being brave. Can you come with us now and help us get an idea of what this blond man looks like?"

Jessica felt dazed. She couldn't believe that they really had to leave Adam there. She shuddered at the thought of his being locked in a cell.

She didn't want to follow the sergeant back to describe the man in the garage. But she knew how important it was to do everything possible to save Adam. And that meant facing, head on, the horrible scene she had witnessed hours before.

"Lizzie, sleep in here with me tonight," Jessica begged her sister. The rest of the family had waited up for Jessica and Mr. Wakefield to return from the police station. They were now completely exhausted.

"There isn't even room for you in here, let alone me," Elizabeth complained, looking at her sister's disheveled bed. One half was piled high with clothes. "I'll be right down the hall. Don't worry." She patted Jessica's hand, but Jessica's eyes were wide with terror.

"Listen," she whispered. "Didn't you hear that?"

"Hear what?" Elizabeth demanded.

"That . . . you know, sort of tapping sound." Jessica was white as a ghost.

"Jess, that's the tree outside tapping against the window. Come on, you're scaring yourself to death."

Jessica didn't answer. Numb with fatigue and fear, she dropped back on her bed, barely noticing when Elizabeth closed the door softly behind her. She could still hear the tapping. The next thing she knew, the room was completely dark, and the tapping was louder. "Jessica." She heard a whisper. "Jessica."

Heart pounding, she sat up in bed. The room was perfectly quiet for an instant, and then—clearly and steadily—the tapping began again. Tap, tap, tap . . . like footsteps. Soft, determined footsteps crossing the foyer to the stairway. "Jessica," a voice rasped. "Help me."

Jessica felt her throat closing with terror. She could hear footsteps on the stairs.

"Help me." Again she heard the low, anguished moan. The footsteps were getting louder. Jessica put her hands over her ears, trying to block out the sounds. The curtains on her window moved in the breeze, and she was sure she saw something moving behind them.

Someone was tapping on the window.

She leaped out of bed and ran to the window. The window was open about four inches, and her first thought was to close and lock it so no one could get in. It was chilly in the room, and a strong breeze was blowing over her as she tried to push down the sash.

But the tapping was getting louder. And then Jessica saw something that made her freeze. A pale hand was struggling to squeeze in beneath the window and the sill, the fingers stretching out as if reaching for something—reaching closer and closer—until they grabbed hold of Jessica's own hand. The icy fingers closed around hers, and she screamed at the top of her lungs.

"Jessica! What is it?" Elizabeth demanded, opening the door and snapping on the lights.

Jessica was sobbing. "The window . . . someone was trying to get in," she stammered. She looked around in confusion. She was fully dressed, sitting on her bed. Nothing was moving at the window but the curtains, which were fluttering slightly in the breeze. "I must've—I guess I was dreaming. I thought someone was trying to get in through the window."

Elizabeth hugged her twin. "Poor thing. You screamed like you'd just seen a monster!"

Jessica didn't answer. She couldn't get the image of those pale, grasping fingers out of her mind. And she knew she wasn't going to fall asleep again that night.

"Liz, I'm frightened," Jessica whispered. "What if that guy tries to find me? He saw me drive off in the Fiat. He knows I'm a witness—maybe the *only* witness."

Elizabeth shuddered. "You'll just have to be careful," she said in a low voice. "Jessica, promise me you'll use your head. If you try to do something stupid, something to impress Seth . . ."

Jessica stared up at the ceiling, her mind racing. She wasn't one bit sleepy. She kept going over and over that moment in the garage. "I can see him perfectly," she said. "His blond hair, that look in his eyes . . ."

"You've got to stop thinking about him. Just rest," Elizabeth pleaded.

Jessica sat straight up, her eyes wide. "What about Adam?" she demanded. "Liz, you don't think he's really mixed up in this, do you? What do we really know about him, anyway?"

Elizabeth shook her head. "I don't know what to think," she said. "But I know you need to get some sleep." She sighed and looked at the rumpled bedding and clothes piled up on the bed. "Want me to stay in here with you?"

Jessica nodded. "Yes," she said softly. "Would you, Liz? I still don't think I'll be able to sleep, but I don't want to be alone."

Elizabeth lifted up the pile of clothes and put them on the floor, then crawled into the bed beside her sister. Elizabeth shivered a little. "I know how you feel," she whispered.

It was hard to believe that just the night before, they had all been perfectly serene—with Adam asleep in Steven's room and Jessica's biggest problem being how to get Seth to pay attention to her. Now it seemed that nothing would ever be simple again. Adam was under surveillance in a cell in the police department. And Laurie Hamilton was dead.

Neither twin could imagine sleeping peacefully again. Not until the horrible crime had been solved and some of the terrible questions plaguing them had been answered.

Jessica arrived at the *News* office exhausted. She had had only a few hours of sleep. Every time she had closed her eyes the night before, she had had a vision of the man in the garage. Even now, she could see his face before her perfectly, and it made her even more acutely aware of how clearly he had seen her.

Seeing Seth again, though, made her feel a

bit better. The news of Laurie Hamilton's murder had hit the office first thing that morning, and reporters were bustling about trying to get the story ready. Seth couldn't wait to pull Jessica aside and find out everything that had happened since he had dropped her off the previous evening. But it wasn't until lunch that they really got a chance to talk. Jessica was disappointed, though, by Seth's initial inclination to believe Adam might have murdered Laurie. After an impassioned speech, she could tell she was beginning to have an effect.

"All right, all right," Seth said, running his hands through his curly hair. "Maybe you've got a point." He stared at Jessica with interest. "Tell me again what this guy Wilson said about the murder weapon."

Jessica took a deep breath. "He said he found a rope wrapped in rags in Adam's glove compartment. It's straight out of Agatha Christie! It's way too obvious," she declared. "Seth, I guarantee you—Adam Maitland is *completely* innocent."

"How long have you known this guy?" Seth demanded. He and Jessica were sitting together at a small table in the cafeteria of the Western Building. Neither of them had much appetite, and the salads they had bought sat untouched before them.

"Look," she said, "I haven't known Adam that long. Steven—that's my older brother—met him in a class this past year at college. But all it takes is one look at the guy to know he's the sweetest, most considerate, most. . . ." Her voice trailed off. "*You* know. He's the sort of guy you want to invite into your home. *Not* the sort of guy who strangles his fiancée."

"He must be going out of his mind," Seth said sympathetically. "Poor guy. Let's just say, for the sake of argument, that you're right, that this guy strangled Laurie and left her body in his car hoping to frame him. Can you imagine—coming out of work late, really tired, opening the trunk of your car and . . ." He shook his head wordlessly. "He must've gone berserk."

Jessica frowned. "What do you mean, 'Let's just say you're right'? Seth, I *know* what I saw. OK, so maybe some of the stories I told you about were a little fishy. I admit it. This is completely different."

"How am I supposed to believe that?" Seth asked. "Jessica, I like you. I think you're a nice girl. But this isn't fun and games we're talking about. This is murder."

Jessica's eyes widened. "I know that. That's why we've got to trust each other, Seth. That's why you've got to believe that I'm telling you the truth!"

Seth sighed heavily. "I'm tempted to believe you. If Adam really is innocent . . ." He stared at her. "Jessica," he said suddenly. "We're going to have our work cut out for us. Do you really want to help crack this case—and figure out who killed Laurie Hamilton?"

Jessica nodded, her eyes still wide. "I really do," she said solemnly.

"Then it's time to get moving. And the first thing to do is to call every single person we can find who knew Laurie—and everyone who knows Adam, too. We've got to learn everything we can about them. For instance, who would want to kill Laurie—and make it look like Adam did it."

Jessica shivered. "Right," she said, getting to her feet.

"Where are you going?" Seth asked, looking down at his untouched lunch. "We haven't started eating yet."

"I don't have time for lunch," Jessica called back over her shoulder. "I want to finish the work I have to do for Sondra so I have more time to devote to our research."

Elizabeth paced around her room, barely noticing the beautiful chamber music playing on her stereo. She was oblivious of everything—

the soft sunlight streaming through the window, the smell of cookies baking downstairs. Everything but the letter in her hand. The letter from Adam.

It was Thursday evening. Adam had been in custody less than forty-eight hours, but it already felt like eons to the Wakefields. And Elizabeth felt it more acutely than anyone else, because none of the others knew what she knew. On Wednesday night she had suddenly remembered the mysterious letter from Adam, and she had been trying to decide what to do about it ever since.

" 'I don't want to hurt her until I have to,' " she said aloud, her fingers trembling. Her eyes dropped down the page to that horrible last sentence. " 'You're all I really want in this whole world, and if I can't figure out something soon, I may have to do something drastic.' " Elizabeth swallowed. She felt dizzy and light-headed every time she looked at the letter. She just couldn't bear thinking that she might have had something to do with Laurie's death.

But suppose that what the police psychologist was saying was true. That Adam, a poor boy from a farmer's family, had gotten all sorts of fancy ideas in his head when he met wealthy people for the first time at college. That he bought things he couldn't afford on credit—like his used car—and didn't know how to get out of debt. That he fell for Laurie because of her money and plotted early on to convince her to marry him secretly, make off with her money when she turned eighteen, and then kill her. That didn't explain why things had backfired—why Adam had killed Laurie now instead of later. Unless . . . and this was the truly horrible part.

Suppose, Elizabeth thought, *she* had been part of the plan. That was what horrified her. She couldn't understand how it had happened, but somehow Adam had fallen in love with her; the letter made that clear. What if he had killed Laurie because he was unable to live with the guilt of loving Elizabeth? She certainly hadn't encouraged him, but that didn't make her feel any better.

She felt that she had no choice. Taking a deep breath, she opened her bedroom door, the letter still in her hand, and headed slowly downstairs. The door to her father's study was closed, and she knocked softly. "Daddy?" she said.

"Come on in, sweetheart," Mr. Wakefield called. "What's up?" he asked, smiling affectionately at her.

Elizabeth bit her lip as she sat down on the edge of a leather chair. "Daddy, you've been a lawyer for a long time," she said slowly.

"Longer than I care to admit!" Mr. Wakefield said cheerfully. "Have you got a legal problem?" he added.

Elizabeth nodded, her eyes filled with tears.

"Looks serious," Mr. Wakefield said. "What is it, Liz?"

"Well, suppose—" Elizabeth began. "Daddy, suppose you had something in your possession that you knew could be used as evidence against someone you liked. But you thought you owed it to—I don't know, I guess to *justice*—to show the authorities the evidence. Would you do it? Even if it could hurt the person a lot?"

Mr. Wakefield studied Elizabeth's distraught expression. "Honey, do you know something about Adam?"

Eyes downcast, Elizabeth nodded.

"If you do, I think there's no question. However much you like him, you have to tell everything you know."

Elizabeth exhaled a long breath. Her hand still trembling, she handed her father Adam's letter.

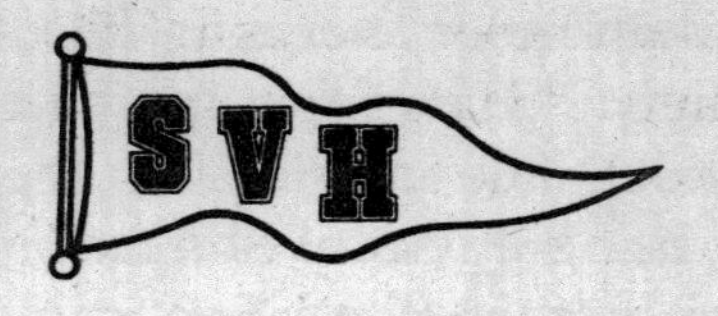

Seven

The atmosphere in the Wakefield household had been so frenetic since Laurie Hamilton's murder that Jessica barely had had time to get her brother Steven alone. For one thing, the telephone kept ringing—mostly reporters calling, asking about the inside story on Adam Maitland. Laurie's death was the biggest scandal to hit Sweet Valley in ages, and the Wakefields were right in the center of it all. Steven was the one who knew Adam best, so he was the one everyone wanted to talk to. By Friday he looked pale and haggard. It was obvious that the combination of working long hours in his father's office and not sleeping at night was beginning to take a toll.

But her brother's health was the last thing on Jessica's mind when she got home from work late Friday afternoon, her arms filled with mindless "homework" given to her by the dreaded Sondra—just a little something to keep her weekend from being any fun! She had been hoping to find her brother alone. She wanted to pump him for information about Adam, and she didn't want anyone else around to get in their way.

"I want to talk to you," she announced without bothering to say hello. Steven was lying flat on his back on a deck chair out by the Wakefields' pool. The late-afternoon sun was still strong at this time of year.

Steven opened one eye and looked warily at her. "Come on, Jess. Can't you see I'm trying to get some rest? I don't feel that great," he added. "And I'm supposed to go over to the police station to see Adam later on."

Jessica brightened perceptibly. "Maybe I'll come with you," she said casually, sitting down on the end of the deck chair.

Steven groaned. "Jess, you know what Dad said. You're supposed to stay *out* of this whole thing. It's bad enough that you might've been a witness. You don't want to make it worse by—"

"By trying to help Adam?" Jessica interrupted indignantly. "Honestly, Steven! I can't believe *you're* talking this way, too." She slumped dejectedly. "And I thought you really cared about what was best for him," she added significantly.

Steven shook his head. "I do," he said. "I'm just not sure what good it can do for you to visit him in jail, that's all." He frowned at her. "Jess, I'm worried about you, I don't want you to put yourself in danger."

"Steven," Jessica said, ignoring his comment, "if we really are going to help Adam, we've got to think hard—we've got to have a plan. Can you think of anyone who hated Adam for any reason? Did he have any enemies at school?"

Steven was quiet for a while. "No," he said at last. "Not that I can think of. Who could possibly hate Adam? He's just a nice, kind, quiet guy from South Dakota. He's always been nice to everyone. The only thing I can think of . . ."

"What?" Jessica prompted him.

"Well, there *was* that guy Laurie knew that Adam mentioned the first night he had dinner with us—the one Laurie's grandfather wanted her to go marry. Adam never talked too much about it. I don't even remember the guy's name. But he did say something once about the guy hating him because they had both fallen for Laurie at the same time."

"Let's go see Adam and ask him about it," Jessica said, jumping to her feet.

Steven shook his head admiringly. "I'll say one thing for you, Jess. When you set your mind to something, you sure don't fool around. Can I at least go and change my clothes first?"

"Sure," Jessica said. She was glad Steven seemed to have forgotten all about leaving her behind.

Adam looked like a completely different person. He had dark shadows under his eyes, and it was obvious that he hadn't slept in days. The police were holding him in a small jail adjoining the station, a temporary holding area for people awaiting trials. He walked out to the small waiting room to meet Jessica and Steven, his eyes on the ground. When he looked up, there was a haunted expression in his eyes that Jessica knew she would never be able to forget.

Steven had been to the police station twice, but this was the first time Jessica had seen Adam since Laurie's body had been discovered. She felt strange. She was afraid to look straight at Adam, afraid he would think she was staring at the faded-gray cotton clothes he was wearing. Prison clothes, she thought with a shudder. Suddenly the reality of the situation became even more apparent. Adam was really in *jail*. If they couldn't find the blond man in the white Trans Am, he might have to *stay* in jail!

"We don't have to keep standing," Steven

said with forced cheerfulness. "Let's sit down." He dragged a wooden chair over for Adam and another for Jessica. With a guard standing at the open door, it wasn't the most private situation, and Jessica felt extremely self-conscious.

"I talked to your parents again today," Steven told Adam. "They're planning to come out here early next week. They said they'd already talked to you, though."

"Yeah," Adam said dully. "I don't think I can face seeing them. I just don't feel up to it."

"You look tired," Steven said, patting him on the shoulder. "You hanging in there? I'm worried about you."

Adam looked away. "All I can think about is that she's dead," he whispered. "I keep trying to tell myself that I've got to make some kind of plan, find a way to get myself out of here. But Laurie's all I can think of. I can't believe I'll never see her again." He buried his face in his hands. "Who would do something like this to us?" he sobbed.

"We're trying to figure out the same thing," Jessica said, her eyes intense. "Adam, Steve and I have been talking about this, and we were wondering if you can think of anyone who could have—" She broke off. "Who could have done it."

Adam flinched. "No," he said softly. "That's what I've been asking myself every single second of the day." He laughed hollowly. "Let me tell you, you sure don't have much else to do in a place like this but think. I can't eat or sleep, that's for sure. I've racked my brain, and I can think of one or two people who weren't that nuts about me—I guess we all have a few enemies—but no one who would've hurt Laurie." His eyes filled with tears. "She was so beautiful, so incredibly sweet, so good-tempered. Who in the world could want to hurt her?"

"I've thought about the fact that it could have just been a horrible coincidence. Maybe some maniac killed her and just chose the closest car—which happened to be yours," Steven said, thinking aloud.

Jessica shook her head. "That's nuts, Steve." She turned back to Adam. "Look, I know how hard it is to talk about this. But the fact is that someone has committed a terrible crime. We've got to find out who did it, before someone else gets hurt."

Adam sagged in the chair. "I just can't see the point," he said dully. "They all think I did it. You should see the way the policemen look at me. And the guards. They've got me starting to doubt everything. Sometimes I even doubt my own sanity!" He shuddered. "It's horrible, being kept here," he added. "But I just don't have the strength to fight it. And now that Laurie's gone, what's the point?" He shrugged listlessly.

Steven and Jessica exchanged stricken glances. "Adam," Jessica said, "you once mentioned a guy Laurie's grandfather wanted her to marry, and Steve said that the guy was upset because you and Laurie fell in love. Do you think he's someone who could hold a grudge—a grudge serious enough to have done something like this?"

Adam was staring down at the floor, his face expressionless. "That was Tom Winslow," he said in a flat voice. "Yeah, he sure hated me all right. His dad and Laurie's grandfather were trying to get the two of them together. Mr. Hamilton didn't care about the fact that Tom was mentally unstable. Tom loved Laurie, though," he added helplessly. "That's the thing—everyone did. I don't think Tom would've intentionally hurt her—no."

"Can you tell us anything more about him?" Jessica pressed.

Adam shook his head. "I'm sorry, Jessica. I'm just so tired," he said faintly. "I just want to lie down." He got to his feet with effort, and in an instant the guard was at his side.

"We'll be back tomorrow!" Steven called after

him, but Adam barely seemed to notice. He just shuffled off behind the guard, as if he hadn't heard.

"Sounds as though he's really going through a rough time, almost like he's in shock," Mr. Wakefield said when Jessica had finished describing what Adam had been like that afternoon.

The Wakefields were trying a new Mexican restaurant in Los Vistas, a town ten miles from Sweet Valley. The family often went out for dinner on Friday evenings when the whole family was at home, but that night no one was very hungry, and most of the food they had ordered sat untouched before them.

"Do you really think so, Dad?" Elizabeth asked.

"Well, imagine what a shock it must be to find yourself thrown into the rigid routine of an institution," Mr. Wakefield replied. "Adam's a country boy, used to fresh air and open spaces. To be locked up like that must be torture."

"Not to mention what he's experiencing after losing Laurie," Mrs. Wakefield pointed out.

"Girls," Mr. Wakefield said, clearing his throat, "this seems as good a time as any to let you know that Sergeant Wilson is concerned about your safety. After all, whoever Jessica saw in the garage saw *her,* too. He also saw the Fiat. Which means he may be looking for you—either of you since he wouldn't know one of you from the other or even that Jessica had a twin."

Elizabeth paled perceptibly. "What are we supposed to do?" she asked a low voice.

"Your father and I would prefer it if you'd leave the Fiat in the garage for the next few weeks. Just till some of this has died down a little," Mrs. Wakefield said.

Jessica looked stricken. "How are we supposed to get anywhere?"

"Well, you could take the bus. Or Steven could drop you off at the *News* on his way to work during the week. Perhaps there's someone there who could bring you back at night," Mrs. Wakefield said.

Seth! Jessica thought. Maybe being banned from the Fiat wasn't as dreadful as it had sounded at first.

"We could always just *paint* it, like they do in movies," she suggested, just to prove she wasn't completely ready to say goodbye, however temporarily, to the car she and her twin shared.

"The car," Mr. Wakefield said, "is to stay at home. Is that understood?"

"Yes, Daddy," the twins said meekly.

"But that isn't all," Mr. Wakefield continued.

"I want you both to promise me you'll use common sense. I don't want to frighten either of you, but I want you to remember: *be careful.* That means never go *anywhere* alone. If you need to get somewhere, you can always call your mother or me, and we'll come and drive you. Be aware of anyone who seems to be trailing you, or of any strange behavior at all, and report it to me at once."

"Dad," Jessica said thoughtfully, "Sergeant Wilson thinks all of these precautions are nuts, doesn't he?"

"What do you mean?" Mr. Wakefield asked.

"Just that I get the feeling he thinks Adam's guilty." Jessica stared down at her untouched dinner. "Why should he worry about what happens to us if he really believes he's got the murderer behind bars?"

"Well," Mr. Wakefield said grimly, "you've heard about innocent until proven guilty, haven't you? Judging by circumstantial evidence, things don't look good for Adam. But Sergeant Wilson is certainly not discounting the possibility that the man you saw, Jessica, is the real murderer. And all of us think that these precautions are necessary for your safety."

Nobody said anything. But Jessica, for one, didn't need any convincing. She was absolutely certain that the man in the garage was going to find her somehow. And she had no intention of going anywhere alone, until this whole mess had been cleared up.

"Things look really bad for Adam," Jessica said mournfully. It was later that evening, and she was in the living room with Steven and Cara Walker, listening to compact discs and trying to decide whether or not to make some popcorn.

Cara, a pretty brunette who was one of Jessica's closest friends as well as Steven's girlfriend, was pacing anxiously. "It's all so horrible," she said. "I wish there was something we could do."

"Yeah," Steven agreed. "It was bad enough before that letter. Now it really looks as if Adam's been lying all along—like he was only going out with Laurie because of her money."

"Letter?" Jessica demanded, her eyes narrowing. "What letter?"

"Liz didn't tell you?" Steven said incredulously. "Boy, that's weird. She was up for a long time last night telling Dad about it. They took it to Sergeant Wilson this morning."

"What letter?" Jessica repeated, her mouth dry.

"It turns out that Adam had an amazing crush

on Liz," Steven said. "He left a love letter under her pillow a day or two after he arrived and poured out his whole heart—told her he loved her, was only sticking with Laurie so he wouldn't hurt her. You can imagine how upset poor Liz was. She felt horrible ratting on Adam, but on the other hand, she could hardly sit on a piece of evidence like that."

Jessica felt a hot flush creep across her face and neck. She couldn't believe it. Elizabeth had taken that letter—*her* letter—to the police? Now Adam was in even deeper trouble, and it was all her fault!

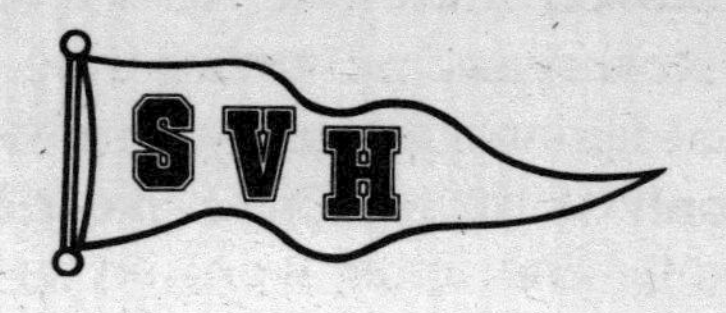

Eight

Jessica stared dully at the front page of the *News*, which was lying next to the computer station she shared with Sondra at the office. The top story of the day was about the Hamilton murder case, as it had been every day since Laurie's body had been discovered the week before. That day's story had a new twist, though. "Letter from Maitland Swears He Never Loved Laurie," the headline ran. The story, written by a young reporter named Dan Weeks, ran as follows:

> A local girl has supplied police with a letter that implicates chief suspect Adam Maitland, 18, in the murder of Laurie Hamilton last Tuesday in Sweet Valley, a police spokesman announced today.

In a typewritten letter to the local girl, a minor whose name police have not disclosed, Maitland allegedly wrote that he no longer loved the victim, 17-year-old Laurie Hamilton. The letter went on to state that Maitland had fallen in love with the girl who received the letter.

"You're all I really want in this whole world, and if I can't figure out something soon, I may have to do something drastic," Maitland allegedly wrote.

Police found Hamilton's body in the trunk of Maitland's car last Tuesday night, after Maitland called them to report the murder. Miss Hamilton, the granddaughter of millionaire Tucker Hamilton, had been strangled. According to police, a rope that may have been used to murder Miss Hamilton was found in the glove compartment of Maitland's car.

Maitland told police he found the body in his car, which was parked in the parking lot of the Western Building, after leaving work at Wells and Wells, a law firm with offices in the building.

Police arrested Maitland Tuesday evening. A trial is scheduled to begin in two weeks.

"This is awful." Jessica groaned and put down the paper. As she glanced at the mountain of data she was supposed to input for Sondra by noon, she frowned.

The work was going to have to wait. She had to go straight to the police department and tell them the truth about that letter.

The weekend had been torture for Jessica. At least a dozen times she had been on the verge of confessing what she had done. First she tried telling Elizabeth, but each time she brought up the letter, or Adam, Elizabeth changed the subject. Clearly her twin was trying to put the whole thing out of her mind. And Jessica found her parents disappointingly uncommunicative as well. Mr. Wakefield frowned when she asked him how much weight the letter would have in court. "It's hard to say," he said vaguely. Even Steven, who had been her closest ally since the whole dreadful mess began, seemed to close up on this issue. It seemed no one wanted to talk about the letter, perhaps because it was the first piece of evidence that forced them to consider something dreadful—that Adam might really be guilty.

All weekend Jessica had mentally practiced her confession. It wasn't the end of the world, was it? So she had forged a letter. It was wrong, but it was better than it would have been if Adam really had written it, right? In a way she would actually look good. Or so she had assured herself when she was alone in her bedroom. But the minute she actually opened her mouth to explain what had happened, she found herself incapable of telling her family what she had done. And now it was Monday morning, and she was no closer to a confession than she had been when Steven had first mentioned that horrible letter on Friday evening. What's more, it was on the front page of the newspaper for everyone to see.

Jessica glanced furtively around her as she slipped out of the computer room, her pocketbook in hand. If Sondra found her sneaking out before she finished her work, she'd lose her internship for good. All she needed was another black mark against her in the Wakefield household that week!

Luckily she made it out of the newspaper office unseen. Once she was outside, she breathed a sigh of relief. She knew exactly what she was going to do now, and it felt as though a great weight had lifted from her shoulders.

Sergeant Wilson looked exhausted. He was sitting behind a huge stack of folders and papers, and from the slightly scratchy sound of his voice and the shadows under his eyes, Jessica had the feeling that he hadn't been getting much sleep lately.

The sergeant asked her if she was Elizabeth of Jessica. After she identified herself, the sergeant asked, "Have you come to see Adam? You know, we really haven't made that much progress. Still no sign of our blond composite or his white Trans Am." He took off his glasses and rubbed his eyes.

"I've come to talk about the case," Jessica said importantly.

Sergeant Wilson raised his eyebrows. "Really? Do you have something new to report to me, young lady? Things don't look too good for your friend Adam now that we've got this letter to consider. . . ." His voice trailed off, and he paused, staring straight ahead with a blank look in his eyes. "I just don't understand it. He really seems to have loved that girl. But that letter. . . ." He shook his head. "Just promise me you'll keep your eyes and ears open."

"You know I'll do anything I can," Jessica said seriously. "I think about that blond guy all the time. I'm so scared I'm going to run into him or that he's following me." She sighed. "Sergeant, I just know Adam isn't guilty!"

Sergeant Wilson rubbed his forehead. "This whole town has gone absolutely nuts since that girl was killed," he said unhappily. "Nothing else on the TV or radio or in the papers. People are desperate to get a verdict. A little, peaceful community like Sweet Valley. I hate to say it, but there's tremendous pressure out there to get Adam Maitland locked up. Tucker Hamilton is a powerful man, and he wants his granddaughter's murder avenged."

"But Adam is innocent!" Jessica cried.

"Look, I understand how you feel," the sergeant said slowly. "But we need proof, Jessica. Solid proof. What have we got to go on but mounting evidence *against* him?"

Jessica leaned forward intently. "I have something to tell you. Something important," she said.

Sergeant Wilson put his fingertips together and waited.

"That letter my sister told you about—the one that's supposedly from Adam. I wrote it," Jessica said hastily.

"You . . ." Sergeant Wilson stared at her. "*You* wrote it? For heaven's sake, *why*?"

Jessica blushed. "Well, it's kind of a complicated story. See, Liz has this boyfriend named Jeffrey French who's a camp counselor this summer in the Bay area. I thought she needed a change. You know, a little variety."

"I don't see the connection," Sergeant Wilson said, staring at her.

"Well, when Steven—my older brother—told us that Adam was moving in, I got this *idea.* I thought it would be really great if Liz and Adam had a little summer fling. I didn't know about Laurie then, and I suggested it to Liz, but she didn't seem all that interested. Then Adam told us about Laurie, and I thought I needed a *plan.*"

"A plan?" Sergeant Wilson repeated in disbelief.

"Yes." Jessica wet her lips. "So I thought about it and decided Liz might be more enthusiastic if she thought Adam loved her. It works in books and on TV all the time," she added defensively.

"So you composed the letter from Adam and typed his name at the bottom of it?" Sergeant Wilson asked.

Jessica nodded sheepishly. "And then I forgot all about it until Steven told me on Friday night that you were planning on using it as evidence."

"Jeez," Sergeant Wilson said, letting out a long sigh. "Here I was, thinking I knew this business inside out. I never—" He broke off and stared at her. "You know," he added slowly, "your testimony isn't going to convince the district attorney. He can easily claim you're lying to protect Adam. And about seeing the blond man, too—after all, no one else saw him. The fact remains that the letter exists—with Adam's name on it. Hamilton is putting a lot of pressure on the DA's office, and he's not going to give up this piece of evidence lightly."

Jessica gave him her most defiant look. "I don't care," she said. "I know it's going to make me look like a jerk, but I'm more than willing to admit I wrote the letter. Even in public."

Sergeant Wilson was quiet for a minute. "Fine," he said. "I appreciate your coming and telling me this, Jessica. But I want to ask you a favor."

"Sure!" Jessica exclaimed, eager to do something to make up for the trouble she had caused.

"Let's keep this letter business quiet," Sergeant Wilson suggested. "You know how quickly things get out of hand, especially in a town as small as ours. I think we can help Adam more by keeping quiet than by trying to defend him outside of court. If what you think is true, *is* really true—that Laurie Hamilton's real murderer is still at large—I think it's to our advantage to keep him from getting nervous. If he thinks we think Adam is guilty, he'll be much more likely not to panic and leave town. So let's let the press and the media keep right on claiming Adam wrote that letter. Does that sound all right to you?"

"Sure," Jessica said. She was beginning to like Sergeant Wilson, and as far as keeping her mouth shut about the letter—well, that suited her just fine. It meant she wouldn't have to get in trouble with Elizabeth, at least not yet. She had already vowed to tell her father about it as soon as possible.

Sergeant Wilson's explanation made sense to her. After all, whoever the guy with the white Trans Am was, it would make sense for him to begin to relax a little, now that Adam really seemed to be taking the blame for Laurie's murder. And Jessica could well understand why the police would see this as an advantage. As far as she could tell, there was only one catch to this plan.

If the man she had seen in the garage was still hanging around, wouldn't he want to feel really secure? And wouldn't he achieve that by trying to get rid of the only witness to his crime?

Seth was in a terrible mood by the time Jessica caught up with him the following afternoon in the *News* cafeteria. He was staring moodily at the chicken fricassee served as that day's entree.

"Hi, Seth!" Jessica said, setting her tray down next to his. She was feeling somewhat better now that the authorities knew the truth about the letter. And it was lunchtime, the only part of the day she could tolerate ever since she had become Sondra's "slave."

Seth took a bite of chicken. "I suppose you know Dan Weeks has suddenly become the hottest journalist at the *News*?" he said. "All because he's been covering what turns out to be the biggest story to hit Sweet Valley in years. *I* could've been covering it if it hadn't been for our little credibility problem last week," he added miserably.

Jessica tasted her chicken, made a face, and pushed her plate away. "I wouldn't worry about Dan Weeks," she said blithely. "I don't think he's anywhere near as good as you are."

"Yeah, well, tell that to Mr. Robb." Seth scowled. "Did you get the memo about this big bash they're throwing on Saturday night? The *News* is having its annual office party, which is probably going to be the worst night of my life. I just *know* everyone's going to be paying all sorts of attention to Weeks, praising him for what a great job he's doing and everything. And I'm going to feel terrible!"

Jessica was quiet for a minute. She *had* seen the memo, but although ordinarily nothing would have pleased her more than the prospect of a party, even an office party, she couldn't get very enthusiastic at this point. "In all the excitement, I'm sure everyone's forgotten about what happened with our story last week," she said. "And sooner or later Mr. Robb will realize you're a much better writer than Dan Weeks. Anyway, about the party. Can you pick me up? My parents won't let Liz or me use the Fiat anymore."

"I guess," Seth said gloomily. He jabbed at the cover story on that day's newspaper. "Just *look* at this, Jessica! This could've been the biggest break of my career."

Jessica opened her milk carton. "That story isn't very well written," she commented. "Look at all the extra words he's got in there! Seth, you're *much* more talented than Dan Weeks."

Seth looked only partly mollified. "What difference does that make? He's the one Robb's assigning to the case, not me. Though it's true I could probably do a better job," he admitted, more to himself than to Jessica.

"Of course you could!" Jessica cried. "Besides," she said, dropping her voice and leaning forward, "I just happen to know that he's got his facts wrong."

"What do you mean?" Seth demanded, his eyes narrowing. At last his attention was riveted on her one hundred percent.

Jessica took her time answering. She was enjoying Seth's discomfort too much to satisfy his curiosity just then.

"Oh," she said casually, "it's just that I happen to know that Adam didn't write that letter, that's all."

Jessica hadn't intended to tell anyone about the letter besides Sergeant Wilson and her father. But she couldn't resist proving to Seth that he had an edge over Dan Weeks—an edge *she* could supply. She felt guilty enough for having hampered his career; the least she could do was to help him out now by making him see how far off the mark Dan was.

Seth stared at her. "Oh, come on," he said at last, clearly not knowing what to think. "If Adam didn't write it, who did? And how could *you* know, anyway?"

Jessica set her milk carton down. "Because," she said calmly, "*I* wrote it, Seth. I wrote it and left it under my sister's pillow with Adam's name on the bottom."

Seth's mouth dropped open. "*You* wrote it?" he said with disbelief. "But why?"

"I'll explain that some other time. Right now I need your help," Jessica said urgently, putting her hand over his. "I've got to help Adam, fast. From what I could tell this morning over at the police station, Wilson is under real pressure to get Adam convicted. He's apparently getting phone calls and letters all the time from irate people who want this case settled. And things are looking bad for Adam. Will you help me try to find this guy with the white Trans Am?"

Seth eyed her wearily. "Isn't that a pretty dangerous proposition? I thought you wanted to hide from him."

Jessica had thought of this already. "Seth, you said you wanted a break—a chance to write the story of the year, even the decade. Well, here it is. Dan Weeks is writing the wrong story. Adam's innocent, Seth. If you really want the facts, you're going to have to help me find them."

"Ok," Seth said grimly. "You're on, Jessica. You've got yourself a partner."

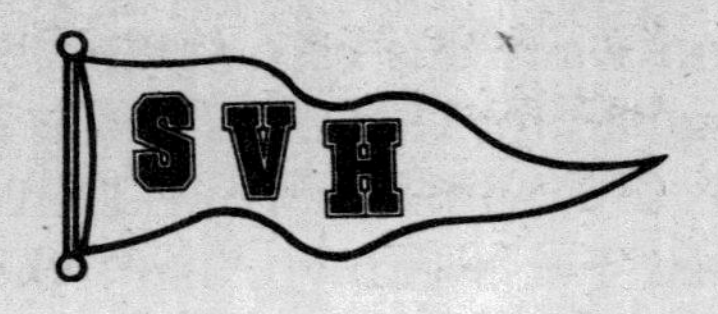

Nine

"As far as I can tell, there's only one tiny little thing we've got to go on," Jessica said to Seth the next day. They were sipping iced tea at a small table in the atrium of the Western Building, trying to come up with a strategy.

"Yeah? What's that?" Seth demanded.

Jessica leaned forward. "Well," she said, dropping her voice conspiratorially, "Steve mentioned something to me about this guy who Laurie was going out with when she met Adam. Steve seemed to think he was pretty bent out of shape that Laurie preferred Adam to him. In fact, Steve couldn't think of anyone else who he could imagine really being Adam's enemy."

Seth frowned. "Well, hasn't anyone asked Adam about this guy? What does his lawyer think?"

Jessica shrugged. "I don't know what his lawyer thinks. But Steve and I asked him about it, and Adam just didn't seem to care. The combination of being locked up and being heartbroken about Laurie seems to be doing him in. He just kind of sits there and stares. He doesn't seem willing to put up a fight anymore."

Seth chewed on the end of his pencil. "That's a real risk in a situation like this. If Adam resigns himself to being convicted, we're in real trouble." He doodled on the pad of paper in front of him. "Got any ideas on how we can snap him out of it and get him to give us something to work with?"

Jessica frowned as she stirred her iced tea. Suddenly she snapped her fingers. "Listen," she said excitedly. "I do have an idea. Maybe if we can get Adam angry—really *furious*—about what happened to Laurie, he'll want to help us do everything we can to track down the guy who did it."

Seth's eyes widened admiringly. "You know, I think I may have misjudged you," he said. "I've got to admit that after everything that happened last week, I thought you were a total flake. But now I see that's not true at all, Jessica."

Jessica lowered her eyes modestly. The truth was she didn't think her plan was half bad. If they could make Adam realize that he was being victimized, if they could get him good and angry and then exploit that anger, it seemed to her that they might get him to help fight his own battle. And at this stage, that was desperately necessary.

Jessica couldn't believe the change that had taken place in Adam's appearance since she had last seen him. After only a week in custody, he bore no resemblance to the boy who had moved into the Wakefield home just a few short weeks ago. He hadn't shaved, and a week's growth of beard covered his face, making it look even thinner. The gray cotton fatigues he had been given by the warden were too big on him, and he looked tired. But more than any actual changes in appearance, what was most striking was how resigned he looked, as if he'd given up on everything. When Seth and Jessica arrived at the police station, Adam was in the small room where visitors were permitted, sitting with a middle-aged couple Jessica guessed must be his parents. The woman dabbed at her eyes as if she had been crying.

"Can we come in?" Jessica asked nervously, not wanting to intrude on the family scene.

"Please do," Mr. Maitland said, getting awkwardly to his feet.

Introductions were made, and Seth and Jessica pulled up two chairs to join the others at the small card table set up in the middle of the room. Jessica noticed that a clock was ticking loudly, and she shivered slightly. It really was a grim atmosphere. She knew the small jail adjoining the police department was only a temporary one, and she could barely fathom how awful a real prison must be.

"Adam," Seth said gently, "I'm a reporter for the *News*, but I'm not officially covering your story. I just wanted to ask you a couple of questions on a strictly unofficial basis."

Adam looked at him dully. "All anyone does is ask me questions. 'Did the police read you your rights? Did you ever plan to do anything about your debts? Did you—' " Tears filled his eyes. "No one ever asks if I miss Laurie, if I can imagine waking up every day of my life knowing she's been murdered."

"Adam, honey, people are only trying to help you," Mrs. Maitland said, putting her hand on his arm.

Adam jerked away as if she had burned him. "No one can help me!" he cried. "Don't you get it, Mom? I've been framed. And whoever did this awful thing is going to get his wish. I'm going to get locked up for good."

"Who would want to do something like that

to you?" Mrs. Maitland cried. "I just can't imagine anything so evil."

Jessica leaned forward intently. "Adam," she said in an urgent voice, "doesn't it drive you crazy, wondering who did it? Don't you just want to get your hands on the person who could have strangled Laurie? How can you stand to be locked up in here when the real murderer is running around free?"

An awful silence hung in the air. Everyone, including Adam's parents, had tried so hard not to mention Laurie's name or to refer to her murder in a way that would upset Adam. But Jessica had purposely made her questions as stark and awful as possible. She watched Adam's face carefully, praying he would have the reaction she hoped for.

At first Adam went dead white. He was breathing heavily and perspiring. His eyes fixed on Jessica's, and for a long, horrible moment he said nothing.

Then he nodded. "Yeah," he said in a tense, angry voice. "I'd like to see whoever it was caught and locked up for the rest of his life."

Seth leaned forward and put his hand on Adam's arm. "Then you've got to help us," he implored him. "Because without you, we're never going to be able to find out who could've done it."

"And that means we won't be able to avenge Laurie's death," Jessica added.

"All right," Adam said. "Tell me what I have to do, and I'll do it."

It took a long time for Seth and Jessica to extract the details about Tom Winslow and Laurie from Adam. He was clearly exhausted, and it wasn't an easy thing for him to talk about. But with some prompting, they were able to get most of the story, in bits and pieces. The Maitlands simply sat quietly and listened.

"I didn't know Winslow very well," Adam began, after Seth and Jessica had prompted him to tell them about Laurie's former boyfriend. "He's a junior at a college up north—a real 'big man on campus' sort of guy. Blond, handsome . . . I guess the sort of guy her grandfather had always wanted for her. On the outside, that is. The truth is that Tom is, and always has been, extremely troubled. He's been under a doctor's care for years because he suffers from severe depression. But Laurie's grandfather didn't seem to care about that. Besides, his father is some sort of hotshot, and he does business with Mr. Hamilton. Anyway, when I met Laurie, she'd only gone out with Tom a couple of times, and only because her grandfather was pressuring her. She liked Tom as a friend—Laurie was such a compassionate girl, I think she really felt sorry for him—but not as anything more."

"So then you two started going out, and Tom was left in the cold, huh?" Seth said when Adam fell quiet.

Adam nodded. "Laurie and I clicked the first time we met. We just had an incredibly good time together. Now that I look back on it, I guess it was a pretty rough situation for Tom. We all felt awkward about it, but Laurie could hardly fake something she didn't feel. And, yeah, I guess Tom was pretty hurt—and upset."

"Did he ever threaten either of you in any way?" Seth asked, looking intently at Adam. "Did he ever give you any indication that he wanted revenge?"

Adam shook his head. "No. He and Laurie had one really ugly scene about two weeks after I met her. I know Laurie felt trapped. On the one hand, she knew she liked me and didn't want anything more to do with Tom. But her grandfather could be terribly strict, and he had made it clear that if she stopped seeing Tom, he'd never forgive her. Laurie was so sensitive about things like that." Adam stopped to clear his throat, visibly trying to keep his emotions in check. "She really loved her grandfather, no matter how impossible he was. I guess Mr.

Hamilton was in the process of trying to close some sort of deal with Tom's father, and the timing was bad. In any case, Laurie went ahead and told Tom she couldn't see him anymore. He was furious. He kept telling her she was an idiot, that she was ruining her life. When he asked her if there was another man, she was honest and said yes. But he didn't ask anything more."

"But he found out it was you, right? I mean, it wouldn't have been too hard," Jessica said. "He must've known that she left him for you."

Adam shrugged. "Maybe. But that was the last either of us heard from him. The person who gave us a really rough time was her grandfather. He started talking about cutting Laurie out of his will. In fact, he made it clear that if she married me, that's exactly what he would've done." Adam laughed bitterly. "Which is why I have such a hard time understanding why the DA's office—and the papers and the news—keep trying to make a link between Laurie's fortune and her murder." He was quiet for a long moment, then said, "God knows what I could possibly have gained from her death. She was the best thing in my life, the best thing that ever happened to me."

Jessica and Seth exchanged glances. "We should go now," Seth murmured. "I think we've tired you out."

Adam looked hard at Jessica. "No, wait," he said, warming up a little. "I have a question or two myself. What's all this about a letter? I feel like I'm really losing my mind. I never wrote a letter to Liz! So who did? How did it get under her pillow? My lawyer keeps assuring me that it's not that strong a piece of evidence, but I don't know. And besides, who could hate me that much? Who would want to frame me?"

"Maybe," Jessica said hastily, not looking at Seth, "it doesn't have anything to do with the murder or framing you. Maybe it's just some kind of mistake." She couldn't tell Adam in front of his parents that she had written the letter.

Seth cleared his throat, and Jessica blushed. Struggling to regain her composure, she turned back to Adam. "Tell me what Tom Winslow looks like."

"Well, he's blond, like I said. Tall—about my height, but broader. He's got very piercing eyes."

Jessica shuddered, remembering the look in the eyes of the man in the garage. The way they had bored into hers. . . . "Have you seen the composite the police have drawn up?" she demanded. "Could it be him?"

Adam frowned. "Yeah, I've seen it, but I'm not sure. I guess it *could* be him," he said doubtfully.

Jessica shivered. "I know he's out there," she whispered. "Adam, will you help us? We've got to find him. I hate to say it, but we've got to find him before he finds us. He knows I saw him that night. He's going to try to find me to make sure I can't talk."

Adam didn't answer for a minute. When he looked up, his eyes were shining with tears. "Look," he said, "I don't know who could have done this awful thing, but of course I want to help you guys find him. I want to make sure he's punished for his crime."

Jessica's heart went out to Adam. But she had to wonder if Seth was thinking the same thing she was: that it still appeared as though they had very little to go on. And for the moment most of the evidence still pointed to Adam.

"Darn," Jessica murmured, glancing at the clock on the wall. Steven and Elizabeth had promised they would be back with Steven's car by five-thirty, and it was already twenty minutes to six. Ordinarily Jessica was the one who kept people waiting. She never wore a wristwatch and tended to be lackadaisical about meeting people on time. But she had sworn to Lila and Amy that she would meet them at the Dairi Burger, a popular hangout, and she knew they wouldn't wait long. Not on a Friday, when they probably had dates lined up that evening. Jessica was eager to get together with her two friends, who had been hounding her night after night on the phone about the intrigue with Adam. She wanted to set the record straight as well as she could. Besides, the Wakefields had practically become celebrities lately. Jessica knew they were counting on her to show up and tell them all how it felt to be on the inside of the biggest scandal ever to hit Sweet Valley.

Jessica's eyes fell on the keys to the Fiat lying on her dresser. They they had been lying there since her father had instituted the "no Fiat" rule after Laurie's murder. She had promised not to use the car, especially not by herself. But her parents were out and wouldn't be back until later that evening. And who knew where Elizabeth and Steven were? All she was going to do was zip over to the Dairi Burger and back again. It seemed insane to miss Lila when the Fiat was sitting right out in the garage. After a moment's deliberation, Jessica swept the keys up and dashed downstairs.

It was still gorgeous and sunny out, and Jessica hummed to herself as she backed the Fiat out of the driveway. She found a good radio station and relaxed as sunlight poured down through the open-topped car. She had forgotten how much fun it was to be in the little Fiat Spider. There was nothing like a red convertible and a beautiful California evening to lift the spirits! Soon Jessica was in a kind of reverie, changing lanes and glancing automatically into the rearview mirror. For the first time since Laurie's murder, she felt almost like her old self. I've really been acting crazy, she admonished herself. From now on she was going to make it a point to spend time with her friends, get away from the claustrophobic atmosphere around the house and the *News office*.

Changing lanes again, she checked her mirror and blinked in surprise. Her heartbeat quickened, and she felt a shiver run up her spine.

A white Trans Am was directly behind her.

Deftly, Jessica maneuvered the Fiat into the right lane, glancing over her shoulder at the car. The driver, a young man, was wearing dark glasses, but he had blond hair.

Jessica was sure he was the man she had seen in the parking deck. She swore under her breath. Had he seen her? Was it possible he was following her?

The next minute the Trans Am pulled up beside her. She saw the S-shaped rust mark on the side door. She was stuck at a red light, so frightened she didn't know what to do. Glancing at him sideways, she saw that he was staring straight ahead and tapping his fingers on his dashboard. He didn't seem to have noticed her, but that could easily have been just an act, Jessica thought. Her hands trembled as she gripped the steering wheel. What should she do? Her first impulse was to turn around and speed home. All she wanted was to get away from that car. But she quickly realized how crazy that would be. If he followed her, he'd find out where she lived. No, the thing to do was drive straight to the police station. That way if he followed her, he would be doing them all a favor!

But when the light changed, the white Trans Am shot forward with amazing speed. Whether or not he had seen her was impossible to say, but it was clear that he was in no mood to hang around.

Still trembling, Jessica turned right at the light and headed back toward the police station. She knew one thing now. The guy she had seen carrying Laurie's body was still around. And the question was, why? It would seem that the obvious thing to do would be to get away immediately.

Unless, Jessica thought weakly, he had a reason for sticking around, such as wanting to find the one person he knew who could convict him.

* * *

"You can't *ground* me," Jessica wailed. "You guys, nobody gets grounded anymore! And don't you think I've been punished enough after the scare I got?"

Jessica and Elizabeth were sitting at the kitchen table with Mr. and Mrs. Wakefield. It was ten o'clock Friday evening, and Elizabeth was listening sympathetically as her twin tried to defend herself. But she could see her sister was fighting a losing battle.

"There's absolutely no reason why you couldn't have waited for your brother and sister to get home," Mr. Wakefield said sternly. "Jessica, this isn't a game. Driving around in the Fiat right now is *dangerous.* Your mother and I were only trying to protect you when we asked you two not to use it until this whole mess has been resolved." He glared at her. "In fact, give me the keys. I'm hiding them until the trial is over. And that's that."

"But, Daddy—" Jessica began.

"No 'buts,' " Mr. Wakefield said firmly. "You are not to leave the house *at all* for an entire week—a week from Monday—except to go to work. Do you understand?"

"Yes, sir," Jessica said, miserable.

Elizabeth raised her eyebrows. This was extremely strict on her father's part. She could tell how upset he was, and she guessed it must be the result of fear. Jessica had scared her and Steven to death, calling from the police station with the news that she thought she might have been followed by the white Trans Am. Steven had driven to the police station and followed Jessica as she drove home, because he had been so concerned. He was the one who had told their parents about the episode.

Elizabeth could hardly believe how much their lives had changed since Adam had been accused of murdering Laurie. It seemed as if fear was part of their day-to-day existence now. True, she had been skeptical at first about Jessica's histrionics. Having been angry with her sister for stretching the truth, if not lying, on several occasions to impress Seth, Elizabeth had not known whether to believe Jessica when she claimed to have seen a blond man carrying a body that horrible night in the parking garage. But it didn't take long before she realized how serious the situation was. Jessica was definitely telling the truth this time. Moreover, Elizabeth couldn't believe the change in her twin. Fun-loving, light-hearted Jessica had become a nervous wreck. She had nightmares almost every night, and every time they approached the garage on the way to work, Jessica was terrified.

Now Elizabeth could sense how alarmed her

father and mother were. Alarmed enough to *ground* Jessica! The Wakefields reserved grounding for the most reprehensible behavior or the most dire emergencies. This was obviously a family emergency, and that's how her parents were handling it.

Elizabeth was just deliberating how Jessica would handle being grounded when the telephone rang. Mr. Wakefield answered it, listened for a moment, then passed the phone to her. "It's someone from the *News*," he said. "I think it's Beth, one of the other interns." Elizabeth took the phone. Beth, a small, pert girl, was working as an intern in the layout and graphic arts department.

"Liz? It's Beth Simmons. Listen, I'm calling to find out if you and Jessica are going to the party at the *News* tomorrow night. I just wondered what time you were going and what you were planning on wearing and everything."

"Uh . . . I guess we're going," Elizabeth said, glancing at her parents and then at Jessica. "Actually, I have to see if it's all right with my parents. Can I call you back and let you know?"

"Sure," Beth said. "And be sure to tell me what you're going to wear."

It took the twins almost half an hour to convince their parents that this was a situation that required relaxing the rules of grounding. Finally the Wakefields relented, under the conditions that the twins leave the house together, stay at the party together, and come home together.

"We promise," Jessica said, the relief of being able to go to the party so evident that Elizabeth almost laughed. "We swear to you that we won't leave each other's sight for one tiny second."

"You'd better believe it," Mr. Wakefield said grimly as Elizabeth hurried back to call Beth. "And remember, this isn't for our good, Jessica. We're trying as hard as we can to alleviate the danger we think both of you may be in right now."

Jessica was unusually subdued. Not even the prospect of the office party, and the chance to spend an informal evening with Seth, appealed to her right then. All she could think about was the white Trans Am and the man inside it. She was almost positive that he had seen her. So Tom Winslow, or whoever he was, was still in town. The question was, how great was the danger he posed?

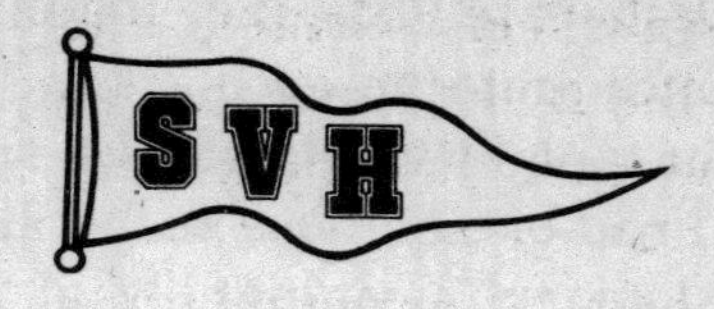

Ten

It was Saturday evening, and Jessica was in her sister's bedroom, inspecting herself in the full-length mirror on the back of Elizabeth's door. Her own room looked like a disaster area, as usual, and there was barely space to turn around, let alone get dressed. Besides, Jessica wanted advice about how to wear her hair.

"I don't see how you can be so excited about this party when Adam's sitting in that prison," Elizabeth complained. "Jessica, don't you think you're being heartless?"

"Absolutely not," Jessica said promptly. The truth was, she was worn out from worrying. What she needed was a break, a chance to have fun. Even if an office party didn't seem like the greatest opportunity, at least Seth was taking them. She and Seth had been so caught up in the Hamilton case that they hadn't had any time to concentrate on each other. Jessica was hoping that tonight would set *that* straight.

"I wish I had one of those leather headbands," she said, looking meaningfully at her sister's dresser, where her brand-new headband was lying. "It would look great with this skirt." She pivoted, admiring the black, slim-cut cotton skirt she was wearing with a white silk T-shirt. She liked the effect—trendy, but professional, she thought. Just the sort of thing to make Seth look at her in a new light.

"You can borrow it if you want," Elizabeth said without interest. "But I still think it's kind of awful, spending all this time and effort getting ready for the party when Adam is in such horrible trouble."

"Liz," Jessica said patiently, "didn't I tell you? Seth and I are going to find the real murderer, and Adam will be just fine!"

"That's great," Elizabeth said dryly. "But the trial is set for a week from Monday, and you don't seem any closer to solving the mystery than you were the day it happened."

"That," Jessica snapped, "just happens to be untrue, Liz." She picked up the headband and slipped it on before her twin could change her mind. "We've got all kinds of clues! In fact, I wouldn't be surprised if we managed to wrap everything up this weekend." She leaned forward to rub a microscopic fleck of mascara from under her eye, her mind clearly on a different issue. "Liz, how long did it take before Jeffrey kissed you? I mean, how long had you guys been friends before you knew he really *liked* you?"

Elizabeth thought for a minute. "Well, remember what a confused mess it all was? I was trying to fix him up with Enid, and you were trying to fix him up with Lila, and I guess it was *weeks* before I realized that I had fallen for him myself—and vice versa."

Jessica frowned as she added a touch of blusher to her cheekbones. "I think Seth may be shy," she hypothesized. "Otherwise, why would he have wasted so many perfectly good opportunities to grab me in his arms and tell me that he loves me passionately?"

Elizabeth laughed. "Good question," she commented. "Poor Seth. Does he have any clue that you're interested in much more than solving the question of who killed Laurie Hamilton?"

"Maybe not yet. But after tonight . . ."

Elizabeth shook her head. "Come on, Jess. It's just a basic office party. All that's going too happen is that Mr. Robb is going to give a little speech, probably sum up the year's work. We'll all have cold drinks and something to eat, and that'll be it. Not the most romantic evening in the world, if you ask me."

Jessica smoothed her hair down. Sometimes she just couldn't understand her sister's lack of imagination. An intimate little office party on a Saturday night seemed incredibly romantic to her. Especially since Seth was driving them there. Maybe Elizabeth could find some other way home from the party, and she and Seth could stop at Miller's Point on the way home to look at the valley lights. In fact, she could deliberately mention it, ask Seth if his family was related to the Miller whom the park was named for. One thing would lead to another, and eventually the moment she had been dying for would finally come. He would look down at her, take her in his arms, and—

"Girls," Mr. Wakefield called, knocking on Elizabeth's door. "We just want to let you know we're leaving now. We'll be over at the Cabots' if you need us for any reason."

"Is Steve gone yet? I wanted to ask him something," Jessica murmured.

"He's gone. Cara picked him up about ten minutes ago. Listen," Mr. Wakefield continued, "I know you've made arrangements to get a ride tonight, but just in the event of a major catastrophe, Steve left the keys to his car on the desk in his bedroom. He said to be careful with the clutch if you use it, he wants to have a mechanic check it out tomorrow."

"We won't need it, Daddy," Jessica said blithely. "Seth is picking us up."

"Remember," Mrs. Wakefield warned, "no matter what, neither one of you is to get into that Fiat."

"Don't worry," the twins said in unison, giving each other looks of mock patience.

"Jeez!" Elizabeth exclaimed when Mr. and Mrs. Wakefield had finally backed the car out of the drive and disappeared. "Sometimes Mom and Dad are unbelievable worrywarts."

Jessica laughed. "That's for sure."

Just then the phone rang. Elizabeth grabbed it, listened for a minute after saying hello, then passed it to Jessica.

"It's Seth," she said.

Jessica snatched the phone eagerly. "Hi," she said, trying to load that single syllable with all the significance she could manage. "How are you?"

Seth sounded harassed. "Jess, I'm really sorry, but you know that piece I was supposed to get Robb yesterday on adult education in Sweet Valley? Well, it still isn't done, and I'm going to have to stay here at the office. I don't think I'm going to be able to pick you and Liz up. Is there any other way you can get to the party tonight?"

Jessica twisted the telephone cord between her fingers. "Seth," she said, "you promised! It won't be any fun unless you can come get us."

"I'm sorry, but Mr. Robb will kill me if this isn't perfect. And after everything that's happened, I don't want to risk another mistake."

Jessica pouted. "Well," she said reluctantly, "I guess we could drive my brother's car over." There went all her plans of getting Seth alone later in the evening.

"Maybe we can all go somewhere after the party," Seth suggested, sounding hurried. "I've got to go now, Jessica. I'm really sorry."

Jessica replaced the receiver. "It's a good thing Steve left us the car keys," she said, "because Seth is working on an article and can't drive us after all."

Elizabeth, who was putting a stamp on a letter for Jeffrey, didn't look overly concerned. "Fine, we'll take Steve's car then. Jessica, remind me to tell Mom and Dad we need more stamps."

Jessica was just on the verge of pouring her heart out about Seth when the phone rang again, and again it was for Jessica. Only this time it was Sergeant Wilson.

"Jessica, I hate to bother you on a Saturday evening, but we've got something over here that we really need you to take a look at. Would you mind dropping by the station for a few minutes tonight?"

Jessica frowned. Things were going from bad to worse. First Seth canceled out, and now she had to go back and be reminded of the whole terrible mess at the station! Not exactly the best way to start what was supposed to have been an evening off.

Suddenly it occurred to Jessica that Sergeant Wilson might want to discuss the letter with her. During her last visit, he mentioned that they would need a signed affidavit to be used in the trial stating that she had written the letter. If that *was* what he had in mind, she certainly didn't want to bring her sister with her to the station. Since she had not told Elizabeth—at least not yet—that she had written the letter, Jessica realized that to keep it secret awhile longer, it would be essential for her to go by the station alone. Which meant that stopping on the way to the party was out of the question.

"I don't really see how I can," she said, turning so her sister wouldn't see her face and guess from her expression that she was trying to hide something. "My sister and I aren't supposed to drive the Fiat, and we're using my brother's car—the only other car at home now—to go over to the Western Building for an office party."

"Who is it, Jess?" Elizabeth demanded.

Jessica ignored her. "Could I come over tomorrow morning?" she asked hopefully.

Sergeant Wilson cleared his throat. "Well, I'll tell you what, Jessica. We actually wouldn't mind getting your opinion about something as soon as possible. So why don't we send over a squad car to pick you up? Then your sister can take your brother's car, and we'll drop you off later on at the party."

Jessica sighed. She was really stuck now! She had no choice but to agree to Sergeant Wilson's plan. She did so, then quietly hung up the phone, still hiding her face from her twin. The prospect of going to the station didn't thrill her, any more than the thought of a police escort to the *News* party!

"What was that about?" Elizabeth asked curiously. "Jess, I'd be happy to stop somewhere on the way to the Western Building if you need to."

"Nah," Jessica said dismissively. "There's no need, Liz." She was struggling to make her voice sound nonchalant. "It was just Sergeant Wilson. They want me to check over the witness report to make sure it's worded right."

"The witness report? What's that?" Elizabeth asked, giving her twin a blank look.

Jessica ran a brush hurriedly through her hair.

"You know, the thing they give to the lawyers," she said vaguely. Before Elizabeth could ask another question, she grabbed her sweater and dashed out of the bedroom. "See you at the party!" she said over her shoulder.

Elizabeth walked slowly over to the banister and watched her sister bound downstairs. "What time are you going to show up?" Elizabeth called after her sister. "And how are you going to get to the Western Building from the station?"

"I should be there by eight-thirty or nine. The police said they'd drive me," Jessica shouted from downstairs. "Make sure and be mysterious about where I am if Seth asks, OK? Tell him I'm getting a ride from another man."

Elizabeth rolled her eyes. She didn't know how Jessica could plot about catching Seth when she was on her way to the police station!

But Elizabeth forgot all about Jessica when the phone rang. She picked it up and heard Jeffrey's familiar voice. Suddenly nothing else mattered.

"OK," Sergeant Wilson said, swiveling around in his chair. "We've got a new composite we'd like to have you take a look at, if you wouldn't mind, Jessica. Our artist has drawn a more complete sketch based on the description you gave us, combined with Adam's description of Tom Winslow. Would you mind telling us if this looks right to you?"

Jessica leaned over the desk and examined the sketch of the young man. Her face was screwed up with concentration as she tried to remember, and suddenly it all came flooding back—the damp smell of the garage, the expression of the man's face when he saw her watching him, the dark green blanket. . . . She shuddered. "That looks like him," she murmured.

"Thank you," Sergeant Wilson said, looking across the room at the two other police officers and jerking his head once. His expression was very serious. "Now, Jessica, we've got a photograph to show you. We want you to look at it *very* carefully before deciding if the man in the picture looks like the man you saw the Tuesday night Laurie was murdered. Do you understand?"

Jessica nodded.

"You don't have to tell us right away. If you have the *slightest* doubt, just say so."

She nodded again. Her palms were damp with perspiration.

Sergeant Wilson took a five-by-seven-inch manila envelope out of his desk drawer, unclasped it, and slipped a photograph out. The silence in the room was oppressive, and Jessica shifted uncomfortably in her chair.

She couldn't tell where the picture had been taken. The man was standing in front of a banner, his face partly obscured by shadow. He was blond and very handsome in a clean-cut, collegiate way. Green eyes, a nice open smile. He was wearing a button-down shirt and a crew-neck sweater.

There was no reason to be frightened, Jessica told herself. It was only a picture. But she would have recognized him anywhere. Her mouth felt dry now, but her hands were so damp she had to wipe them on the sides of her skirt.

"That's him," she said. "That's the guy I saw that night in the garage."

"Jessica," Sergeant Wilson said, leaning forward intently to peer at her face, "are you *absolutely* sure?"

Jessica nodded. Her heart was beginning to beat faster, the way it had when she had spotted the white Trans Am behind her the other day.

"Absolutely," she said faintly. "That's the guy."

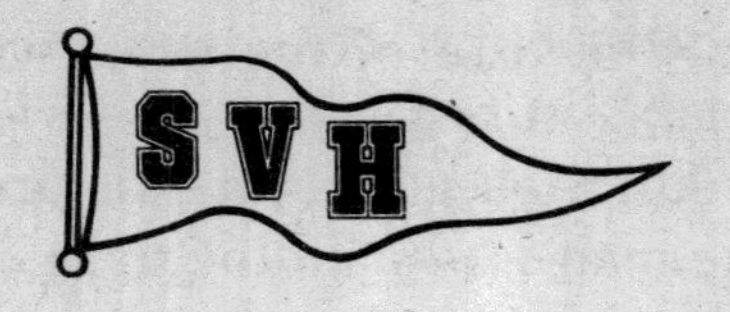

Eleven

Elizabeth checked herself in her mirror, not really paying that much attention to her reflection. Her mind was buzzing with recent events, which were all the more vivid for having described the latest details to Jeffrey on the phone. After telling him the story, Elizabeth felt more certain than ever that Adam was innocent. She had never really doubted it for a second, although she had been taken aback when she remembered his letter.

But there was something fishy about that letter. She wasn't sure what, but it just didn't sound right. The writing was too stilted to have been written by someone tormented enough to be thinking about breaking off an engagement. Not that Elizabeth could be completely sure of that. She didn't know Adam that well. But she sensed that the tone of the letter was wrong. Was it possible that Tom Winslow *had* written the letter, had somehow gotten into the Wakefields' house? Elizabeth shivered at the thought.

"Boy, this place is quiet!" she said suddenly, pausing when she thought she heard footsteps on the stairs. She shivered and then laughed at herself. "I'm getting as bad as Jessica—jumping at my own shadow," she murmured. Gathering up her pocketbook and a jacket, she hurried out to Steven's car, closing the back door firmly and locking it behind her.

It was a beautiful evening, and once she was outside, Elizabeth's uneasiness dissipated. She couldn't help thinking how strangely her twin had been acting since Laurie Hamilton had been killed. But Jessica had been more like her old self tonight, she reminded herself. She had been excited about the party. If only the police hadn't called to remind her of the murder all over again! Elizabeth's one hope was that Jessica would have a good time at the party that evening. The poor thing really needed to forget all about the crime she had witnessed—at least for one evening.

While she was thinking about this, Elizabeth took the keys to her brother's car out of her pocket and opened the door on the driver's side. Well, she thought philosophically, all they could hope for now was that the police could track down the real murderer. She couldn't believe Adam had any real part in the tragedy, and her heart almost broke when she tried to imagine what he must be going through.

At least his parents were around to help comfort him. Elizabeth had only spoken to the Maitlands on a few occasions, but she could tell what warm, loving people they were. They would be doing everything for Adam they could.

Elizabeth slid into the driver's seat and turned the key in the ignition. She heard a clicking noise and nothing else. What had Steven said about the clutch? She tried the ignition again, and again heard nothing but a clicking sound. The engine wouldn't turn over.

"Darn it," she said, glancing at her watch. It was almost nine o'clock. She had planned on being at the party by eight-thirty. She shouldn't have stayed on the phone so long with Jeffrey.

"Come on, car," she said encouragingly, giving the dashboard a little pat. She took a deep breath, turned the key in the ignition, and tapped the gas pedal the way she had seen her brother do when the car wouldn't start. But it didn't help. The car wouldn't budge.

"Well, I guess that leaves the good old Sweet Valley Taxi Service," Elizabeth said out loud, getting out of the Volkswagen and hunting in her pocketbook for her house key. She glanced sidelong at the Fiat as she headed back inside. It really seemed nuts to pay ten dollars for a cab when the Fiat was sitting right there. But a promise was a promise, and Elizabeth knew her parents would be upset if either she or Jessica went back on their word.

It was five minutes past nine by the time she got hold of the taxi company, whose line had been busy the first two times she called. Elizabeth tapped her fingers impatiently on the counter. She didn't want to be late to the party; it wouldn't look very good, and this job was something she cared about enormously. She still hoped Mr. Robb would let her write her own feature piece by the end of the summer. How impressive would it look if she didn't show up on time for the office party?

At last someone answered. "I wonder if I could get a cab," Elizabeth began.

But the woman cut her off almost at once. "We're completely booked up for the next forty-five minutes. We've only got three cabs tonight, and it seems all of a sudden everyone in this town needs a taxi."

"Oh," Elizabeth said, nonplussed. "Thank you anyway." She hung up and glanced at the clock on the kitchen wall. Well, so much for trying that, she thought unhappily. Now what? She could take the bus, but that would take ages.

You are not going to use the Fiat, she instructed herself fiercely. *Absolutely not!* Personally, Elizabeth didn't see what was so dangerous about it, and in fact the longer she stood there in the kitchen, car keys dangling from her hand, the more frustrating the whole situation became. But a promise was a promise. She dialed Enid Rollins's number, thinking that perhaps Enid would be able to give her a ride to the party. But the answering machine picked up on the fourth ring.

It seemed that the only alternative was to walk down to the bus stop. Sighing, Elizabeth went back outside, determined to try Steven's car one last time, but she couldn't get it started. As she sat in the driver's seat, it occurred to her that it wasn't the greatest idea to walk down to the bus stop all by herself on a Saturday night. Hadn't her parents made them swear not to go anywhere by themselves? Which meant—and Elizabeth really *did* think she was being perfectly reasonable about this—that she was stuck having to break a promise either way.

Or miss the office party altogether and risk disappointing Mr. Robb.

No, she had to go. The question was, which was safer: walking alone on the dark, quiet streets to the bus stop or hopping in the Fiat and driving—doors locked, of course—straight to the Western Building?

The answer seemed obvious to Elizabeth. Without another moment's thought, she leaped out of her brother's car, hurried back into the house, and began to search for the keys to the Fiat. Where would her father have hidden them? It took several minutes, but at last Elizabeth thought of the special enameled box her father kept on the desk in his study. He often put important things in there. Sure enough, there the keys were. If she really hurried, she could still get to the party before she was unreasonably late. She dashed out to the garage, unlocked the Fiat, and started up the engine.

It was twenty minutes past nine. If she hurried, she wouldn't be *that* much later than she had promised Jessica earlier that evening.

Sergeant Wilson himself had given Jessica a ride to the Western Building earlier that evening.

"Jessica," he said as they drove, "I want you to do me a favor. Promise to keep everything we've talked about tonight very quiet, OK? I think it'll make our work a little easier if you can do that."

"Sure," Jessica said. She had goose bumps on her arms, and her mouth felt dry. She looked up at the lit windows on the fifth floor of the Western Building, where the party was being held. Only one entrance to the main office building was open after hours, and that was through the garage. The thought of walking alone through that dark garage terrified her, but she was too embarrassed to ask Sergeant Wilson to come in with her.

"Uh . . . thanks for the ride," she muttered, hoping to stall him.

Sergeant Wilson glanced down at his watch. "Thank *you*," he said promptly. "You've been a big help to us, Jessica. I feel certain that we're going to locate Tom Winslow very soon and solve this case."

Jessica swallowed nervously. Well, this was it. She screwed up all her courage and slid out of the squad car, then slammed the door shut. She gave the sergeant the bravest goodbye wave she could muster.

Take deep breaths, she said to herself as she opened the door to the parking garage and looked around her uneasily. The garage was seven stories tall—the same height as the Western Building. The parking floors were designed on a spiral structure, with the elevator banks in the center, near the glass guard booths. As Jessica hurried across the cement floor of the ground level to the elevator banks, she was relieved to see a guard in the booth. She promised herself that after her internship at the *News* ended, she wasn't ever coming back here—unless she absolutely had to.

She shivered as she stepped inside the elevator, then pushed five. She couldn't wait to be inside the *News* offices. *What's taking the stupid elevator so long?* she thought as it went up. She was shaking by the time the elevator stopped and the doors slipped open. The familiar blue columns made her heart sink. How she hated this place! Any excitement she had felt earlier about the office party had vanished during the talk she had had with Sergeant Wilson. Now she just wanted to hurry up and get this evening over with. She certainly didn't want to be walking alone through this parking garage.

Jessica took a deep breath as she gauged the distance between her and the brightly lit entrance to the Western Building several dozen yards away. Almost despite herself, her eyes flew to the spot where—

Don't think about it, she urged herself. But the image was too strong to suppress. She squeezed her eyes tightly shut, and it all came flooding back to her: the sound of something crashing at the far end of the garage; the swishing sound of cloth against cloth; a trunk banging shut; footsteps; and that terrible, indelible image of the man staggering under his dreadful load.

Jessica's eyes flew open as she walked as quickly as possible down the main aisle toward the building entrance, trying to control her fear. She was less than ten yards from the door when she spotted a white Trans Am parked in aisle J, three spaces away from the front entrance.

"It can't be," she whispered, staring at the car. She felt frozen to the spot—an expression she had always thought stupid, but which proved just then to be true. It was as if she couldn't move, however much she wanted to run.

Maybe . . . maybe it's not the same car, she thought to herself, trying to squelch her rising terror. At the same time she was thinking, *what if it is? What if he's been following me?*

She felt dizzy with fear. She stumbled as she raced toward the entrance of the building, almost falling down before she caught herself. She only looked back at the car once. And there it was—that weird rust stain, more like a backward Z than an S. It was the same car all right. Jessica tore at the handles of the entrance doors.

All she wanted was to get inside, where there were lights and people.

The car was empty. The obvious question was: Where was the driver?

By the time Jessica got inside, it was after nine, and the office party was in full swing. A makeshift bar had been set up in the computer room, and dozens of *News* employees were sipping drinks and listening to music provided by a disc jockey. Jessica set her jacket down at a free table and looked anxiously around for Seth. She wanted to call the police right away, but she was so scared, she wasn't really thinking straight yet. Somehow the thought of finding Seth, and alerting him to the fact that the Trans Am was out there, seemed crucial. She really needed his moral support. Her eyes picked out a number of familiar faces but no Seth.

Then she caught sight of him, over near the bar. In her haste to get to him, Jessica almost knocked over a chair, but she barely even noticed. All she could think of was getting Seth to come with her to call the police. They had to get Sergeant Wilson to come back here right away, before the Trans Am disappeared. And where was the driver? Jessica wondered. Was Tom Winslow—or whomever—somewhere in the Western Building? Seth would know what to do. At this point Jessica was so shaken that she was afraid she might burst into tears.

Seth was deep in conversation with a man with blond hair whom Jessica didn't recognize from the back. She rushed up behind him, gesturing frantically at Seth to get his attention. "Seth!" she exclaimed. "You've absolutely got to help me. You're never in a million years going to believe—"

At that point the man turned around, and Jessica froze. Her mouth dropped open in horror, and she broke off in the middle of her sentence. In her confusion she lurched forward, bumping into him and making him spill some of his drink.

"I'm sorry," she said, turning beet red. She didn't want to meet his eyes.

"It's all right. Don't worry about it," the young man said pleasantly, his green eyes fixed curiously on hers. *As if he's trying to place where he's seen me before,* Jessica thought. She grabbed hold of the bar to steady herself.

There was no doubt about it. He was the man from the garage—the same man she had tried so hard to describe over and over again to the police.

"Where've you been? I thought you'd be here

ages ago," Seth said, giving her an affectionate pat on the arm.

Jessica's eyes were wide with terror. "Uh, I had to . . . uh, talk to someone," she muttered. She couldn't look at the blond man. Her heart was beating so loudly, she was sure they could both hear it. Did he recognize her? Why was he staring at her like that? "Seth," she said in a low voice, "can I talk to you for a second? I've got a question to ask you about your piece on adult education."

"Sure, but let me introduce you first to Thomas. His father and Bob Carlisle were college roommates."

Jessica couldn't believe her ears. Bob Carlisle was the sports editor. She couldn't believe what a mess she was in. Tom . . . Thomas. Could this be Tom Winslow? Jessica could only concentrate on one thing—Thomas's penetrating eyes. How long would it be before he recognized her?

"It's—it's nice to meet you," Jessica murmured.

"The pleasure," Thomas said seriously, taking her hand in his, "is all mine." He fixed his eyes on her intently.

"I never knew he was a friend of Bob's," Seth confided in Jessica as they moved away together, leaving Thomas looking after them curiously.

"I've seen him around before, but I didn't realize—"

"Seth," Jessica demanded in a stage whisper, "don't you know who that is?"

Seth stared. "Of course, I just told you. His father is a good friend of Bob Carlisle's. His father is some sort of industrial whiz, and they're really loaded, but Thomas isn't one bit pretentious. He's—"

"Seth," Jessica said, her face dead white, "I don't know what his name is or who his father is, but I know one thing. Whoever that guy is, he's the one who murdered Laurie Hamilton."

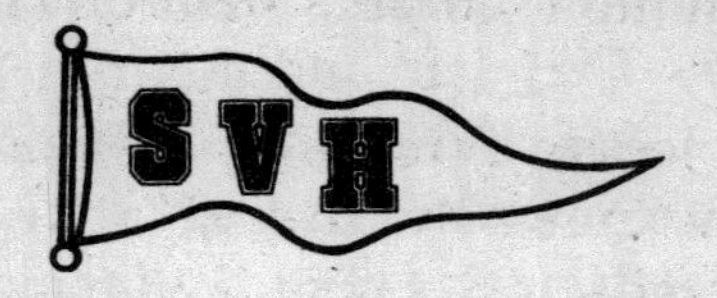

Twelve

Seth narrowed his eyes incredulously. "What?" he cried. "Jessica, what are you talking about? I told you, Tom Winslow is the son of a good friend of Carlisle's. I hardly think he can be the same guy you saw in the garage the night of the murder. I've got to tell you, Jess, I'm beginning to doubt your sanity. First you make up that stuff about arson at the Box Tree Cafe, then you get me to write up a totally false article about stolen money that your neighbor buried in the yard. I believe that you saw *someone* in the garage that night, but you can't expect me to believe that Tom, this nice guy who Carlisle introduced me to personally, is a murderer. Come on, Jess."

"Seth, you've got to believe me. I'll never forget that face as long as I live. And besides, I just saw a photograph of him down at the police station. That man and the man I saw in the garage are one and the same, I promise." By now Jessica was white as a ghost and breathing heavily. "Seth, we've got to call the police. *Right now!*"

Seeing her reaction, Seth realized she wasn't making up a story. "OK, OK. Calm down, Jess," Seth said, setting his drink down and staring across the room at Thomas, who looked perfectly at ease. "The thing to do is act normal, Jess. Don't let him see how flustered you are. I'm sure he didn't recognize you. If he did, he'd be getting out of here as fast as he could." His eyes still on Thomas, Seth picked his drink up and took a small sip. "Now here's what we're going to do. You stay right where you are, and whatever you do, act natural. Understand? I'm going to slip out of here and call the police. It'd be too risky to call from one of the office phones. Mr. Carlisle might decide to show Thomas around."

"Don't leave me here alone with him!" Jessica gasped.

"Just act natural," Seth whispered urgently. "Jess, the most essential thing is to keep him here at all costs. We can't let him get out the door!"

"But if he talks to me again and if he looks at

me again, I know he's going to figure it out!" Jessica cried.

Seth set his drink back down, his eyes still on Thomas. With his right hand he groped in his pocket for change. "You'll be all right," he said, "as long as you stay at the party. I'm going. And remember, stay absolutely calm. If he comes back to talk to you, whatever you do, don't panic."

That, Jessica thought desperately, was the craziest thing Seth had ever said to her. How was she supposed to keep from panicking when she was trapped in this newsroom with the man she was convinced had murdered Laurie Hamilton? Any minute Thomas was going to remember why she looked so familiar. And what was she supposed to do then?

Seth had been gone less than a minute when Thomas turned and crossed the room to join Jessica. Heart pounding, Jessica tried her hardest to keep her composure.

"Bob never told me that the *News* had hired anyone as beautiful as you for the intern program," Thomas said in a low voice, still staring at her.

Jessica spun around, spilling half the soda she had just poured herself, and turning bright red.

Thomas raised an eyebrow as she fumbled for a napkin to wipe off her arm. "I always make a point of asking Bob if anyone *interesting* has come to the *News*," he continued in the same smooth, sophisticated voice. He shook his head, making a little *tsk-tsk* sound. "I'll have to give him a talking to."

Jessica bit her lip. *Just act normal,* she told herself firmly. *Whatever you do, you can't let on that you recognize him.* In fact, it was becoming apparent to Jessica that he didn't recognize her. And actually, that made sense. It had been fairly dark in the garage, and he had been intent on his horrible task. By the time he'd been aware that she had seen him, she was in the Fiat. It was probably the Fiat that had impressed itself on him. Unless he was an extraordinary actor, she couldn't believe he knew who she was. He was too calm, too self-possessed.

Knowing this, Jessica relaxed enough to set down her dripping glass and get a good look at him. He was a little shorter than she remembered, about five-foot-nine, with thick blond hair that touched the top of his collar. Under any other circumstances, Jessica would have found him handsome. He had a strong, square jaw and piercing dark green eyes. He had a good build, too, which was emphasized by his tailored, European-style clothes. All in all he looked clean-cut and respectable—so respectable, in fact, that Jessica was beginning to wonder if she was nuts. Could this be the wrong guy? No. The coincidence was too great. She had seen the white Trans Am, and now she'd seen him. It all fit together too well.

"You know," Thomas said, eyeing her closely, "you look kind of familiar to me. I keep thinking I know you from somewhere."

"Oh," Jessica said hastily, "people tell me that all the time." She inched away from him and glanced wildly about the room for some excuse to break off their conversation. "Do you know what time it is? I'm waiting for my sister to show up. Maybe I should give her a call," she mumbled.

"Hmmm. I *definitely* know you from somewhere," Thomas said decisively. He crossed his arms, studied her face, and it suddenly occurred to Jessica that he was flirting with her. "Let's figure out where it could be. Do you go to school around here?"

"I go to high school," Jessica said pointedly. "Something tells me we wouldn't have crossed paths there."

Smiling, Thomas rocked back and forth slightly on his heels. This seemed to be a game he liked, and Jessica's barbed rebuttal only spurred him on. "All right, let's think where else it could have been. What about the club? Do you play tennis?"

"No," Jessica lied. Actually, she was an accomplished tennis player, but she didn't want to encourage Thomas. She wanted Elizabeth to arrive so they could figure out what to do.

Thomas snapped his fingers. "I've got it!" he cried. Jessica stared at him uneasily. Could this be it? Would he be stupid enough to announce out loud that he'd seen her in the garage the night of Laurie Hamilton's murder? She held her breath.

"The sailboat races at Martin's Bluff last spring. Weren't you part of the crew for a boat called *Lone Blue*?"

"No," she said, letting out a sigh of relief. "No, I've never been sailing. So, your family and the Carlisles are friendly?"

"Yes. My mother is trying to convince me to come and work for him when I finish college, but I'm not too interested in the newspaper world. It's always struck me as being a little too grubby, if you know what I mean." He flicked an invisible speck of dust from his jacket.

Jessica swallowed. She was finding it harder and harder to remain calm. She could hardly believe she was in the same room, face to face with Laurie's murderer, chatting easily and making small talk. This was insane. Where was Seth? What could possibly be taking him so long at the phones? She knew she wouldn't be able to keep up this act much longer.

"Hey, I have a great idea," Thomas said suddenly, showing brilliant white teeth when he smiled at her. She thought he had a horrible smile, much more like a leer. "Why don't we get out of this boring party and go some place a little more intimate?" He lowered his voice. "I happen to know a great little pub around the corner. You can tell me all about how a beautiful girl like you has ended up as a gofer in this boring place."

"I—uh, I really can't," Jessica said, trying to keep her cool.

"Look," Tom said, sounding impatient, "this party is a drag. Are you going to come with me or aren't you? I don't think I can stand to stick around here another minute."

Jessica started. "I've got to stay," she said. "Remember, I *work* here." Her tone was ruder than she had intended, but at least Thomas got the message. He stalked off without another word.

Suddenly Jessica realized what a stupid thing she had done. If Thomas left just then, chances were he'd disappear. She needed to stall him, to keep him there until the police arrived.

"Thomas!" she called urgently, racing after him.

He turned back, a sullen look on his face. "What is it?"

"I just remembered," Jessica said, "where we may have met each other."

His eyes darkened. "Oh, where?" he asked suspiciously.

"Well, it was about a year ago at the—" Suddenly her dreadful attempt to detain him was interrupted.

"Jessica, there's a phone call for you," Beth Simmons said. "I think it's your brother."

Jessica didn't know whether to be relieved for an excuse to finally leave Tom or terrified that he would get away in her absence. "Excuse me for a minute, Thomas. Promise me you'll stay," she begged him as she backed off.

Jessica picked up the phone in a nearby office. Now that she was alone, she noticed that she was trembling violently and her throat was dry. "Steven?" she said.

"Jess," Steven said, sounding upset, "Cara and I just came back to the house to pick up something, and I saw the Fiat's gone. Did you or Liz take it over to the office? My car is still in the garage, and I don't know what's going on, but Dad's going to have a fit if one of you took that car out."

Jessica paled. "Oh, no," she moaned. "Steven, Liz must not have been able to start your car. Do you think she would've taken the Fiat?"

"Dad's going to kill her," Steven said flatly. "You'd better tell her to turn around the minute she gets there."

Jessica was staring at Thomas through the doorway of the office. Something so unimaginably horrible had just occurred to her that she could barely speak. "Steven," she said in a low, urgent voice, "we're in trouble here. Tom Winslow is at this party. I'm trying to keep him here until Seth can get the police." Her voice shook. "Steve, I don't think he recognizes me, but if he leaves, if he's in the garage when Liz drives up in the Fiat. . . ." She felt so shaken by the thought, she had to sit down. "I know he'll recognize the car. Oh, Steve. He's going to find her. What are we going to to do?"

"Well, Jessica," Mr. Robb said, coming over to join the distraught blonde at the bar, where she was trying desperately to keep up some kind of conversation with Thomas. "I see you've managed to find Tom." He glanced at his watch. "But where's your sister? Didn't you come together?"

Jessica eyed the clock frantically. She had been wondering exactly the same thing. The seconds were ticking by, and she could tell Thomas was dying to leave. He had already mentioned it twice. The thought of Liz driving into the Western garage in the Fiat was agonizing. "I'm sure she'll be here any minute," she murmured.

Mr. Robb patted Thomas on the shoulder. "I'm glad you could come tonight, Tom," he said. "Doesn't being here in the office make you want to reconsider joining the newspaper business? It's been incredible around here lately. This Hamilton murder has kept us all here around the clock." He sipped his drink. "Boy, I'll tell you, I've been an editor at this paper for over ten years, and I've never before watched a series of stories emerging that so depressed me about human nature."

Jessica felt her throat tighten. She couldn't believe Mr. Robb was talking about the murder right in front of Thomas. She was afraid to look up and see his expression.

"Well," Thomas said stiffly, "it's been great to see you, sir, but I promised my folks I'd stop by and see them before ten. I really think I should get going."

"But the party's just beginning!" Mr. Robb cried. "I really want you to meet Dan Weeks, the young reporter who's been covering the murder case. He's right over there in the corner now. Won't you just come over with me and say hello? I think Weeks is one of the finest young guys we've got, and the stuff he's turning up—"

"I'm sorry, but I really have to go," Tom repeated. "Thanks, anyway. Would you say goodbye to Bob for me?" He turned to Jessica. "I'm leaving," he said grimly. "Would you like to come with me?"

"Uh . . ." Jessica stared at him. She had no idea what to say.

"Well, do what you want," Tom said, turning on his heel and walking toward the door.

"Tom, wait!" Jessica gasped, starting after him. She couldn't bear the thought of going alone with him out to that terrible garage. But what if Elizabeth showed up just when he was leaving? If he saw the Fiat . . .

She couldn't go out to the garage without Seth. But Seth still hadn't come back from the pay phone, and there wasn't a single minute to lose.

Elizabeth pulled the Fiat into the first floor of the garage. She decided it would be most convenient to drive up to the fifth floor and park right near the entrance to the *News* office. She couldn't believe it was already nine-thirty. She just hoped she hadn't missed the best part of the party. And she hoped Jessica wasn't upset with her for being late.

To her surprise, the fifth floor was full. There were more people at the party than she had thought. She was just about to circle up to level six when she saw headlights shining at the end of aisle J. Someone was about to leave.

"Thank goodness," Elizabeth said. She drove slowly down aisle I, turned at the corner, and pulled up just short of the car that was pulling out so that she could wait for the spot.

Elizabeth was thinking distractedly about the *News* and what the party would be like—thinking too hard to notice that the car was a white Trans Am and that the driver, a clean-cut blond man in a tweed jacket, was staring at her, an expression of horror on his handsome face.

Thirteen

Elizabeth backed the Fiat into the space left by the white car, anxious to park and get into the party before it got any later. She unbuckled her seat belt, took the keys out of the ignition, and was about to open the car door when she realized something peculiar had happened.

Instead of driving away after he pulled out, the man in the white car had stopped directly in front of the Fiat as if he were trying to block her from driving away. Elizabeth squinted. It was fairly dim in the garage, and she couldn't make out his features. In any case, she didn't want to climb out of the car while he was sitting there. She honked her horn twice, assuming he was looking for something in the glove compartment and would step on the gas in a minute.

Then she saw the S-shaped rust mark on the side of the car.

"OK," she told herself, a deafening roar flooding her ears, "the thing to do is stay absolutely calm. He's probably just sitting here for a second, and he has no idea who I am."

But her growing terror told her otherwise. What an idiot she'd been to take the Fiat! It was possible he might not have gotten a good enough look at Jessica to remember her face, but the red Fiat Spider was an instant giveaway. Now Elizabeth was in it, and the guy who had murdered Laurie Hamilton had her trapped!

Elizabeth leaned on the horn with all her might as the blond man opened the door of his car and strolled toward her, a menacing look on his face. She started to roll up the window, but he stuck his hand in before she could get it completely closed.

"I don't suppose you'd care to explain how you managed to get from the party out here to this cute little car in a matter of seconds?" he said in a harsh voice.

"I, uh . . ." Elizabeth stammered, trying to clear her head.

"I didn't recognize you at first," he continued, his green eyes filled with contempt. "I guess you thought I was pretty stupid, didn't you? Tom Winslow isn't very quick on the draw these days. Is that what you were thinking?"

Omigod, Elizabeth thought with horror. *He thinks I'm Jessica.*

Elizabeth had never been so frightened in her life. Her hands were cold and clammy on the steering wheel. She was having great difficulty breathing, and the roaring in her ears was growing louder and louder. She tried desperately to think straight. She had to get out of the car somehow. Tom stepped even closer, and her heart pounded so hard she thought she might faint.

Tom leaned forward and looked at her with a mixture of fascination and hatred. "You know, I've got to hand it to you, Jessica. You really gave me the runaround in there. First you acted like I was the scum of the earth, not even good enough to smile at when I said hello. Then you started to act as if you really liked me." He reached his hand all the way inside the car and touched Elizabeth's hair. She jerked back involuntarily.

"Don't like that, huh?" he said in a sinister voice. "I guess it's one thing when there're a lot of people around, and another when we're out here, just the two of us."

Elizabeth's eyes filled with tears. She glanced desperately around her, trying to seize on a way to escape. If she could slip into the passenger seat and get out before he could cut her off . . .

"Don't make it hard for me, Jessica," Tom said in an ugly voice. Crouching down, he picked up a large piece of lead pipe from the garage floor and raised it menacingly.

Elizabeth's eyes widened with terror. The lead pipe was over a foot long and broken at the end. Tom inched closer, gripping the pipe with both hands and staring at the windshield of the Fiat. The glass was all that protected her from him, and suddenly it seemed unbelievably fragile. She couldn't take her eyes off that piece of pipe. *He's a crazy man, a murderer,* she realized with horror. *God knows what he might do to me.*

"Just sit tight," Tom said evenly, his eyes fixed on hers, "and we won't have to do anything nasty. You understand me?"

Elizabeth nodded dumbly. She was too terrified to say a word.

"Now," Tom said in a cold, even voice, "I want you to get out of the car on *this* side. I'm going to help you. You put your arm out first, and I'm going to give you a hand." He laughed malevolently. "You wouldn't want to trip, fall down, and hurt yourself or anything."

Elizabeth wet her lips. "Where are you taking me?" she asked.

"You'll see," Tom said. He looked away for a second. "You know," he added, almost softly, "I've never really had a girlfriend, Jessica. I loved a girl once, but she didn't love me back. You know what it feels like to love someone who barely even notices you're alive?"

Elizabeth swallowed. This was it. As soon as Tom got her out of the Fiat, there would be nothing between them, nothing between her and the pipe. He still held it threateningly over-head. This was the minute to try something drastic.

Leaning forward, she pressed both her fists into the horn of the Fiat. The loud sound seemed to echo endlessly around the cavernous garage.

"Stop that! Cut it out!" Tom screamed, losing his cool completely. He smashed the lead pipe into the windshield, cracking the glass. Elizabeth turned the key in the ignition, put the car into drive, and gunned forward, smashing into the side of the Trans Am. She wasn't even sure what she was trying to do. She just knew she had to get away.

But Tom wasn't going to let that happen. Elizabeth heard a terrible series of crashes as Tom pounded on the sides of the car with the pipe. Choking with terrified sobs, Elizabeth opened the front door, put her arms up and cried out to him to stop.

"I promise I'll do whatever you want," she cried in a shuddering voice. "Please stop."

"Hold it!" a voice cried out. Alerted by the noise, the security guard had raced over. He was clutching an old tire iron in his hands as a weapon. Now he inched toward Tom. "Drop that pipe," he said in a low voice. "Drop it—right now."

With one amazing leap, Tom jumped toward the guard, tackled him and knocked him down, sending the tire iron flying across the cement floor. The guard, knocked out by the fall, lay motionless, and Elizabeth covered her face and moaned.

Tom was still waving the pipe, a maniacal look in his eyes. "Get over here," he said roughly. Elizabeth's knees were trembling, but she moved toward him, too frightened not to obey. The next thing she knew, Tom was twisting her arm behind her back and holding her pinned to the side of the Fiat. She could feel his hot breath on the back of her neck. Then he pushed her forward violently until her head hit the top of the car with a terrible crack. Elizabeth cried out at the sharp pain, then slumped forward, unconscious, against the car.

Jessica ran down the corridor toward the double doors leading out to the garage. She didn't know where Seth was, but she knew she couldn't wait another minute. She had to chase Tom Winslow. The thought that Elizabeth might be driving into the garage in the Fiat, that Tom might find her, filled her with dread. How had she managed to get her twin in such terrible danger?

As she hurried through the corridor of the Western Building, she heard a horn honking, then a series of crashing sounds. Jessica instantly broke into a run and threw open the heavy double doors that led to the garage.

"Elizabeth!" she cried as loudly as she could, "Liz, hang on! I'm coming!"

Heart pounding furiously, she charged off in the direction of the crashing noises. She felt certain that her sister was in mortal danger. *Just let Liz be all right,* she prayed. *If Liz is all right, then nothing else matters.*

What she saw when she rounded a corner made her heart stop.

Tom had Elizabeth forced up against the side of the Fiat. He had twisted her left arm behind her as he pushed her face forward, causing her to strike her head against the top of the car. The blow clearly knocked Elizabeth out, for she slumped forward and went limp.

Jessica's mouth dropped open. She was so frightened, she didn't think she would be able to move. Her mouth shaped the word *Liz,* but no sound came out.

Quivering with fear, she inched forward. Just then her foot struck something hard, and she looked down to see a rusted tire iron on the garage floor. Without stopping to think, she picked it up. It was then that she saw the guard lying several yards away, still unconscious. Jessica tightened her grip on the tire iron. She was going to need it.

Without conscious plan, she dropped down into a crouching position, the tire iron under her arm. From this position behind Tom, she could creep forward stealthily without him seeing her. Inching forward bit by bit, she waited until she was almost upon him. As he spun around at the sound of her approach, she clutched the tire iron in her hands like a baseball bat and swung with all her might. The tool struck him on the side of his head.

Tom moaned in agony, reeled from the impact, then fell down on his knees on the garage floor, clutching his head. The iron had cut a jagged wound on his right temple.

Jessica ran over to her sister, who was still slumped over the car. "Liz," she cried, turning her around and touching her face. A huge bump had risen on the front of her head, and she moaned at Jessica's touch.

"Liz, wake up," Jessica cried, patting her firmly on the cheeks. She shook her gently, her fear growing.

Tom was still conscious, and there was no telling how long it would be before he managed to come after them again. She had to revive Elizabeth and get her out of the garage. There wasn't a second to lose!

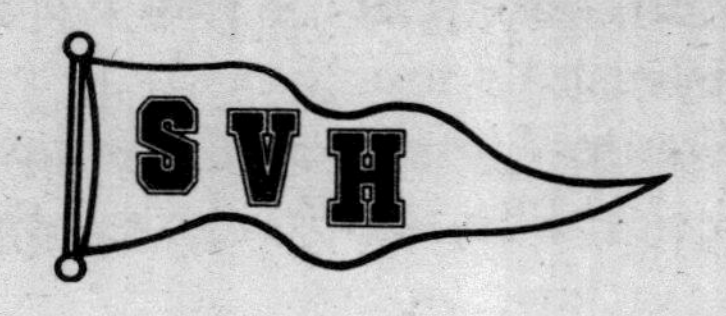

Fourteen

"Wh-where am I?" Elizabeth stammered, staring up at her twin in total confusion.

"Oh, Liz, thank God you're coming to!" Jessica cried. "Can you stand up? We've got to get out of here quickly."

Elizabeth groaned and pressed her hand to her forehead. "My head," she murmured. "Jess, what's wrong with my head?"

"Tom knocked you out. Can you walk, Liz? We've got to go. *Now,*" Jessica said urgently.

Elizabeth's eyes registered terror as flashes of the horrible scene she had endured came back to her. "Where is he?" she asked, trying to lift her head.

Jessica put her arm around her sister and hoisted her up to a standing position. "Don't look," she ordered her twin. "I clubbed him with that tire iron, but I guess I didn't do it hard enough."

Elizabeth's gaze immediately flew to the spot where Tom was kneeling, clutching his bloody forehead and grunting in pain. The sight sent adrenaline pumping through her veins. "Come on," she gasped, staggering. "Let's get out of here. We've got to get the police!"

"I'll hold you up. Just make sure you don't fall," Jessica instructed her. And with her arm supporting Liz, she tried to hurry them both along. They were almost as far as the guard booth when they heard Tom's chilling voice behind them.

"Take one more step," he said icily, "and I'll bash your heads in." He rubbed his eyes. "God knows why there're two of you, but I'll get you both," he said menacingly.

The twins froze.

"Turn around, both of you," Tom ordered. When they obliged, he went on in his threatening, icy voice. "Now walk toward me, *slowly*."

Jessica met her sister's horrified glance as they inched their way toward the crazed young man. She could see her own terror mirrored in Elizabeth's face. Tom was the most gruesome, frightening sight she had ever seen. She felt her knees buckle as she tried to focus on him. The spot where she had hit him with the tire iron was swollen and bleeding badly. But the most frightening thing about Tom's appearance was the expression of deadly calm on his face.

"What are we going to do?" Elizabeth whispered out of the side of her mouth.

Tom moved forward, the lead pipe in his hands. He gripped it so tightly it trembled.

"We've just got to run," Jessica hissed. "Try to make it to the door. You go first, and I'll come after you."

The glass door to the stairs was about ten yards from them. Jessica's glance flew back and forth from their current position to the door. If they could make it, they would have the door between them.

"I'm not sure I can move very fast," Elizabeth whispered back.

"Try your hardest," Jessica urged. "I'm going to confuse him." She glanced anxiously at the door. "And when you get past the door, try to get help—fast. I'm going to need it."

"OK," Elizabeth muttered. "Tell me when."

"Go!" Jessica said, giving her a little push.

As Elizabeth started for the door, Jessica lunged forward, trying to wrest the weapon from Tom's hand. Tom, astonished, wounded, and completely dazed, took several seconds to grasp what was happening. His immediate instinct—to strike out with the pipe—was hampered by Jessica, who had managed to pin his arm behind his back.

"You little idiot," he muttered, jerking his arm free and lifting the lead pipe. He inched toward her again. "I'm going to bash your head in, you hear me?"

Jessica stared past him, completely numb with relief as she realized that Elizabeth had made it to the stairs in time. She backed away, holding her hands out in front of her.

"I promise not to give you any more trouble," she said weakly. "Honestly, Tom. Whatever you want me to do, I'll do."

"Just shut up," Tom said roughly, jumping forward and grabbing her. "I've heard enough out of you. In fact, I think it's just about time I shut you up for good."

Elizabeth's head was swimming. She didn't know how she had managed to find the strength to run the distance to the stairs. She could hear Tom shouting, and she was trembling violently. He could be hurting Jessica! She had to get help. And fast.

Just then Elizabeth's eyes fell on the fire alarm on the wall of the stairwell. She wrenched off her shoe and broke the glass case, then pulled on the lever. The entire garage began to reverberate with the loud, pulsating alarm. Elizabeth slumped against the railing of the stairwell, trying to clear her head. She had to get back out there and save Jessica. But her head was throbbing so badly. The next thing she knew, she was slipping back into darkness, and she sank down to her knees in a faint.

"This way! It's coming from here!" Seth Miller called, racing ahead of the others into the garage. "Over toward the center aisle, near the guard booth!"

"Just step back, son," one of the security guards shouted, racing ahead of Seth toward the guard booth. "Who's supposed to be on duty here?" he demanded, pointing to the empty booth.

"George," the other guard said. "Look! There he is! He's been knocked out," he cried, dropping down beside the man and rolling him over. "He's alive, but he's suffered a bad blow. Someone call an ambulance."

The group rounded the bend and froze in horror at the scene before them. Tom, bleeding and staggering, was lifting the pipe over Jessica's head, clutching her arm tightly to keep her still.

"Let go of her!" Seth screamed, racing forward and knocking the pipe out of Tom's hand. The next minute Seth was on top of Tom on the garage floor, pinning him down. One of the security guards raced over with rope to tie Tom's hands together, and the other hurried over to Jessica, who was almost incoherent with terror.

"My sister," she gasped at last. "I think she's in trouble. She's in the stairwell."

"The police should be here any second," Seth said once the guards had Tom under control. "I called them ten minutes ago, and they said a squad car was on the way." He glared at Tom. "I guess we've finally got the real killer."

The relief of being rescued hit Jessica all at once, and she began to cry.

Seth lifted her gently in his arms. "Are you all right?" he asked tenderly, brushing her hair away from her forehead. "Jeez, Jessica, you've been so brave. I can't believe what you've been through. Do you realize what you've done? You caught the murderer."

Jessica looked at him in a daze. The ordeal she had been through was still too painfully vivid to sort out. Now, she just wanted to make sure her sister was all right.

An hour later the twins, Seth, Mr. Robb, Cara,

and Steven were sitting in the police station, waiting for Sergeant Wilson to finish reading Thomas's rights to him. Steven and Cara had arrived on the scene just as Thomas was being taken away in a police car.

"You have the right to call a lawyer," Sergeant Wilson said. "And you have the right to remain silent. A grand jury will be considering the indictment at once, and until such time, you are to remain in custody."

Tom stared at the ground, silent. A large white bandage covered the place where Jessica had hit him with the tire iron.

As the guards led Tom away, Sergeant Wilson folded his arms across his chest, looked after Tom, and said, "Well, I guess it's been a pretty wild evening for you two girls. Are you both all right?"

The twins nodded.

"Liz got hit pretty hard on the head and passed out," Jessica said. "But you're OK now, right?" she asked her sister anxiously.

"I'm fine," Elizabeth said. "It was awful! Just when I most needed to help you, my legs turned to mush."

"Well," the sergeant said, "we'll need to get formal statements from you, but we'll get it over with as quickly as possible. You girls both need a good night's sleep to help you recover from this whole mess."

"Sergeant Wilson," Elizabeth said in a low voice, "what about Adam? Will he be able to come back home now?"

"He certainly will. Now that we've gotten the real murderer, Adam Maitland will soon be a free man—thanks to the two of you." He flashed the girls a big smile.

Jessica sank back in her chair, a tiny smile on her face. She had to admit that now that it was all over, she really *had* behaved heroically. And she didn't feel one bit bad about the fact that everyone was praising her. Catching a murderer, now that the murderer was safely behind bars, had been unbelievably exciting.

And best of all, Seth was finally paying attention to her.

"Mr. Robb," she said, never one to let a good opportunity pass her by, "it looks like we're going to have to work incredibly hard to get the *real* story out on the Laurie Hamilton murder case. Don't you think Seth would do a wonderful job with it?"

Mr. Robb looked at Seth. "You might be right, young lady. What do you say, Seth? You think you're up to it? It's going to be the hottest story of the decade, and so far we're the only ones who know about it."

"Of course," Jessica continued sweetly, "Seth would never want to take *all* the credit. He'd want some help, someone to work with. Someone who really knows what happened from the inside out. Someone like *me*."

The enormous smile that had been spreading across Seth's face began to fade. "Jessica, you're not even a reporter," he objected.

"Seth," Mr. Robb said reprovingly, "that doesn't seem like a very nice thing to say—especially after everything Jessica's been through tonight." He tapped his fingers thoughtfully on the table. "In fact, I think a collaborative story is kind of a nice idea. We've never done it in the past, but that doesn't seem like a good enough reason not to do it now. Jessica," he concluded with a smile, "you're on. No more computer work for you. You and Seth will be completely in charge of covering the Tom Winslow story. Who knows," he added. "You may discover you work really well together as a team."

Mr. and Mrs. Wakefield weren't home yet when the twins, Cara, and Steven got home.

Elizabeth was actually glad to have this moment to be alone with her sister. She followed

Jessica into the kitchen and sat down, while Cara and Steven went into the living room.

"Jessica Wakefield, I can't believe you," she cried. "Only *you* could take a disaster like this and turn it around so everything works out exactly the way you want it to!"

"What do you mean?" Jessica asked innocently, turning the kettle on. "I'm making you some herbal tea, Lizzie. You still don't look right to me. I think that blow to your head really did a number on you."

"It isn't my head!" Elizabeth retorted. "I happen to have wanted to write a story of my own all summer. What I want to know is how *you* came out of this whole mess looking like a hero, and managing to get everything you wanted!"

"Liz," Jessica said solemnly, "we've got to stop bickering and think about more important things, such as how we're going to explain to Mom and Dad that you drove the Fiat tonight."

Elizabeth paled. "Darn. I forgot all about the Fiat. It's going to need a lot of work. Tom bashed it in with that pipe, and I hit his car when I was trying to get away. And then I just left it in the garage when Steve and Cara drove us over to the station!"

"What station?" their father's voice boomed as the back door opened and Mr. Wakefield entered the kitchen, followed by Mrs. Wake-field and Steven. "And where's the Fiat?"

Mrs. Wakefield took one look at the swelling on Elizabeth's forehead and paled. "Liz, what happened?"

"Hi, everyone," the twins said at the same time. They exchanged apprehensive glances, and Jessica leaned over to give her sister's hand a reassuring pat. She couldn't help being glad it was Elizabeth who had broken the rule about the Fiat this time.

"Are you two all right?" Mr. Wakefield asked. "What's going on, anyway?"

Neither twin answered, then both started to speak at once.

"It was a disaster," Jessica declared.

"We've got a lot to tell you," Elizabeth said.

"But we think you should all sit down first," Jessica pressed, pouring her mother a cup of tea and handing it to her. When everyone was seated, she proceeded to fill them in on the highlights of that evening's traumatic events.

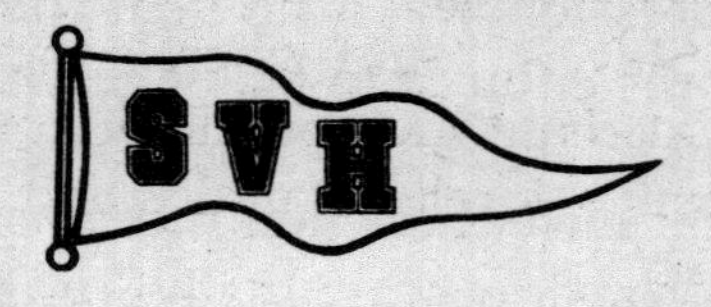

Fifteen

Everyone in the Wakefield household slept late on Sunday morning. They were completely worn out from the hysteria that had ensued once Jessica had finished her brief report of Saturday evening's events. Mr. Wakefield had been on the phone for hours afterward, calling Adam's parents to tell them that Winslow had been arrested, calling Adam's lawyer to see how quickly Adam could be released, and trying to reach Sergeant Wilson at the station to learn more information. Elizabeth slept soundly, and when she woke up, sunlight streaming through her open window and the cheerful sound of sprinklers whirring outside, she almost forgot what she and Jessica had been through. Then it all came back to her in a rush, and she shivered, in spite of the sunlight. Just picturing

Tom's expression when he held that pipe over her head was enough to make her stomach turn over. Frankly, Elizabeth knew she would feel much better once the whole story had come out and Tom Winslow was finally locked up—and Adam was released from that awful jail.

"Adam's parents are coming over for tea this afternoon," Mr. Wakefield was explaining when Elizabeth padded down to the cheery Spanish-tiled kitchen where the whole family was eating breakfast.

"How are you feeling, dear?" Mrs. Wakefield asked with concern, scrutinizing the swelling on Elizabeth's forehead.

"Fine. My head's a little sore, but otherwise fine."

"You guys are real heroes," Steven said, helping himself to a fresh cranberry muffin. "I'll bet Adam and his parents will be grateful to you for the rest of their lives."

Jessica swallowed a spoonful of grapefruit. "I can't wait to start working on the story," she announced.

Elizabeth groaned. Obviously Jessica had another candidate for eternal gratefulness, and it wasn't one of the Maitlands. Poor Seth, she thought. He probably thought the real danger was over—little did he know it was just about to begin!

"Would you guys mind if I called Jeffrey long distance this afternoon?" Elizabeth asked her parents. "I'll pay you back when the phone bill comes. I just really want to talk to him."

"Of course, sweetheart. Go right ahead," Mrs. Wakefield said. She smiled at her daughters. "You girls have both been through a real ordeal. It's probably going to take you a few days to recover."

"I don't need to recover," Jessica said blithely, opening the morning paper and looking with smug satisfaction at Dan Weeks's leading story on the Hamilton murder. "Suspect Still Held in Murder Trial—No New Evidence Found," the headline ran. Just wait, Jessica thought happily, until she and Seth got their story together and revealed what had really happened!

"You know," Steven said thoughtfully, "there's one part of the puzzle that still doesn't seem to fit. OK, let's suppose that it all happened the way it looks, that Winslow was bonkers, essentially, and tried to frame Adam and get rid of Laurie at the same time. That still doesn't explain why Adam wrote that letter to Liz."

A tense silence followed Steven's statement. Jessica squirmed and stared down at her plate. Mr. Wakefield cleared his throat. When Jessica had finally told her father what she had done, he left it up to her to decide whether or not to confess she had written the letter to Elizabeth, and he could see now that she had chosen the path of least resistance.

Elizabeth looked thoughtful. "That's true," she said.

"It could just be a coincidence," Jessica said hastily. "What's the big deal? Suppose Adam just *happened* to have had a crush on Elizabeth and then this whole mess happened and it made him look like a criminal?"

"Yeah," Steven said, taking another muffin, "but that still doesn't make sense. Would Adam had been so unbelievably devastated over Laurie's murder if he'd secretly fallen in love with Liz?"

Elizabeth stared at her twin as a terrible thought occurred to her. "As far as I remember," she said slowly, "there was only *one* person who hoped Adam was going to fall in love with me this summer. And it wasn't Adam."

No one spoke for a moment, and Jessica's discomfort intensified. "Well," she said at last with forced cheerfulness, "that was a great breakfast, but I think I'd better get moving. Seth and I are going to get started on the story today. I'm meeting him at the office."

"Jessica," Elizabeth said, "I don't suppose there's anything *you* happen to know about that letter that you feel like telling the rest of us, is there?"

Jessica glanced unhappily at her father, then at her sister. If only her father weren't sitting there with that knowing look on his face! She could hardly lie in front of him. But this wasn't exactly the way she had hoped Elizabeth would find out. She really had intended to confess, eventually—once it was all so far behind them that Elizabeth would be bound to forgive her.

"I—uh, well—" she stammered. "Look, can we talk about this later? You know what it's like at the paper. They need this story out *right* away."

"Jessica," Elizabeth shrieked. "Do you mean *you* wrote that letter and left it under my pillow?"

"I didn't say that." Jessica jumped to her feet and looked longingly at the door. "Liz, can't we talk about this later?"

"I can't believe you!" Elizabeth cried, her face reddening with anger. "That is the lowest, most contemptible, *vilest*—" Her voice broke off as she stared at her twin.

"Most loathsome," Steven contributed helpfully.

Stricken, Jessica turned to her father for help. But no assistance seemed to be coming from that quarter. "I've got to go," she said weakly. "But, listen, before you guys are ready to put me in the cell next to Tom Winslow's, let me just say this in my defense. I *did* confess to Daddy, and to the police, that I'd written the letter. So Adam didn't take the rap for it. At least the police and the lawyers knew."

"But what about the stories in the paper?" Elizabeth cried. "Jess, Adam has every right to be furious with you. Maybe even to sue you. When I think what could've happened if you hadn't caught Tom . . ."

"But I *did* catch Tom," Jessica said triumphantly. "In fact, I think you're wrong about Adam. I don't think he's going to be one bit angry with me. And if you and Steven want to spoil his homecoming by dragging that silly letter into the conversation, that's your problem. I happen to think Adam will be *much* too grateful to waste his time harping on details." Head held high, Jessica flounced to the door. Without waiting for further objections, she walked right out the door, pleased with the dramatic exit she had created.

"Only Jessica," Elizabeth said, shaking her head as she watched her twin leave, "could manage to make me feel bad for criticizing her for something *she* did wrong!"

"Well," Mr. Wakefield said cheerfully, "that's what sisters are for, Liz. At least you haven't managed to damage her self-esteem!"

"You can say that again," Steven said. "Something tells me by the time Jessica finishes writing this story, we'll have to build onto the house to make room for her swollen head!"

Elizabeth sighed. She didn't feel willing to brush off Jessica's letter. In fact, the more she thought about it, the angrier it made her.

Jessica and Seth spent three hours that afternoon at the station interviewing people—first Sergeant Wilson, then the lawyers, and finally Adam, whose parents were with him, helping him get his belongings together and signing release forms. They were all heading over to the Wakefields' later that afternoon, and Adam was going to stay with his parents at the hotel until they left for South Dakota the next day.

The talk at the station was all about Tom Winslow.

"Frankly, we're expecting him to plead insanity," Sergeant Wilson confided to Jessica and Seth. "Thomas Winslow is clearly an unstable young man."

"And what about Adam?" Jessica asked.

"Now that Tom has confessed, the charges against Adam have been dropped. He's free to leave this afternoon."

Seth and Jessica exchanged glances. "Well,"

Jessica said, getting to her feet, "it looks like we'd better get back to the office. Have we ever got a story to write!"

"You're not kidding," Seth said excitedly, putting his notebook in the breast pocket of his jacket. They each shook hands with the sergeant and thanked him for all his help, then said their goodbyes to Adam and his family, promising to see them back at the house later that afternoon. Five minutes later they were in Seth's red Celica, heading back to the Western Building.

"This garage is going to give me the creeps for ages," Jessica confided as they parked the car on the fifth floor of the parking structure.

"I've got to hand it to you, Jess. You really are brave," Seth said admiringly as they walked toward the doors.

Jessica's eyes shone. "Brave enough to deserve a dedication in your next mystery?" she asked him.

"I always wondered how you knew I write mysteries," Seth said. "No one at the office knows except Mr. Robb."

"Listen, Lester Ames," Jessica said mischievously, slipping her arm through his, "don't think you're the only one around here who knows how to be a sleuth. If I can solve the biggest murder in Sweet Valley's history, why are you so surprised that I happen to know you write mysteries?"

Seth shrugged. "I guess," he said lightly, "I've got a lot to learn about you, that's all."

Jessica hid a smile. That was the understatement of the year.

"Hey, Seth," she said huskily, letting her fingers drop onto his as they entered the office building together, "weren't you absolutely *terrified* about me last night? I mean when you came into the garage and saw Tom holding that pipe and everything?"

Seth swallowed. "Yeah, I was pretty scared," he admitted.

"I'll bet you were afraid you'd never get to tell me how you feel about me," Jessica went on, her eyes never leaving his. "You knew that I'd end up getting killed just trying to insure that *you'd* have a really good story to write. I guess you were really impressed with how devoted I was to you."

"Well, I didn't exactly—"

"You see, that was the whole reason I was risking my life," Jessica continued solemnly. "I couldn't bear to think that I'd jeopardized your career by giving you that false lead awhile ago. So I swore to myself that whatever it took, I was going to make it up to you. And I did, didn't I?"

"Uh, yes. You did," Seth said uncertainly.

"Well!" Jessica said. "I guessed we've cleared that up. The other thing I was wondering about is when you were going to tell me how sorry you were for not believing me at first when I told you who Tom was."

Seth reddened. "I meant to say something about that," he admitted. "I'm sorry, Jessica," he said sincerely. "Will you let me do something to show you how sorry I am? Can I take you out to dinner or something?"

"Well . . ." Jessica said, pretending to think it over. "I guess so. But wouldn't you like to do something else for me?"

"What else?" Seth said gloomily. "I'll take you out to the best restaurant in Sweet Valley. I'll do anything. Just tell me what you want."

"Write your next mystery about me," Jessica said quickly. "You can change my name if you have to, but make sure you leave enough stuff in so my friends know it's me, all right? And make sure I'm the heroine."

Seth groaned. "*Jessica—*" he objected.

"Or else I suppose I could just tell Mr. Robb that I don't think it's very fair for you to get to write this story when you were so suspicious about it all along," Jessica said thoughtfully, watching as Seth unlocked the door to the *News* offices.

"All right," Seth said, relenting. "You win. The next Lester Ames mystery will have you for its star, somehow." He sighed. "You sure drive a hard bargain, you know that?"

Jessica grinned. She knew that. She also knew that Seth hadn't heard all her demands yet. For example, she had every intention of finding out what it felt like to be kissed by a published mystery writer. After all she and Seth had been through, she wasn't sure if the spark was still there.

But there was only one way to find out. And working late hours together on this story would give them plenty of opportunities!

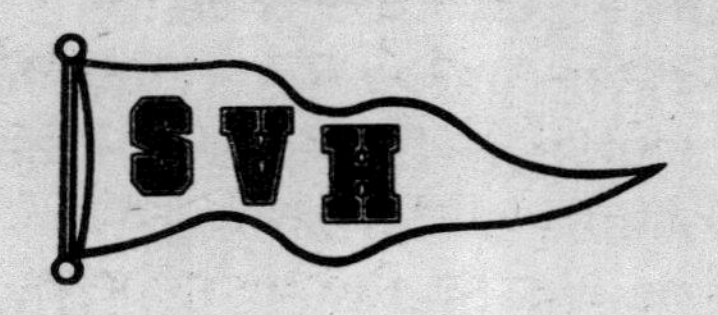

Sixteen

"This whole thing has been such a nightmare, it's hard for me to know what to think," Adam said slowly. He was sitting outside on the Wakefields' deck, looking thoughtfully at the group around him. Elizabeth thought she could see tears in his eyes. "I guess going through something like this makes you realize that what really matters in life is your friends and family," he added in a choked voice. "I could never have gotten through any of this without you guys to support me."

"Bad as it was for us, we didn't have to suffer anywhere near what you did," his mother said softly, patting him on the arm. "We know you're still suffering, Adam. No one can set right what happened to Laurie."

Adam stiffened slightly. "You know," he murmured, "it's always going to hurt, hearing her name. I guess . . . I don't know, when I was a little boy I used to think there was nothing in the world that could go wrong that you or Dad couldn't fix. Maybe the worst part of growing up is realizing that some things that go wrong *can't* be fixed. No," he added, shaking his head. "Nothing can bring Laurie back."

"But, Adam," Mr. Wakefield said, leaning forward, an intent, serious expression on his face, "there may not be anything that can undo the horrible tragedy that has occurred. That's true. But there is something that can be done. And I want to tell you that everything that's happened since the day you moved into our house has reminded me of why I made one of the most important decisions of my life when I was your age."

"What's that, sir?" Adam asked.

"To study law," Mr. Wakefield replied. "Remember the first night you came, when we sat out here eating dinner and you talked about working for Wells and Wells and what going to law school would mean to you? It brought back such memories!"

"I don't know," Steven said. "I bet you must hate the thought of going back to Wells and Wells now," he added, turning to Adam. "Probably the last thing you want to think about is criminal law."

"No," Adam said seriously. "Your father is right. The legal system can't bring Laurie back, but it *can* make sure that Tom Winslow is kept from hurting other innocent people. In the end that's the most important thing. I know it'll be hard for me to go back to work, but it would be much worse if I couldn't."

Mrs. Maitland dabbed her eyes. "I'm so proud of you," she whispered.

"I'm proud of you, too, Adam," Mr. Wakefield said, his voice emotional. "It takes a rare kind of person to go through what you have, with your strength and conviction. I think we've all learned a great deal from your example."

"You know," Adam said softly, "something very special happened to me this afternoon. You guys had gone outside to wait for me," he told his parents, "and I was still in the police station, signing the last forms and getting my things together. Anyway, the door opened and in walked Tucker Hamilton. I can't even remember the last time I saw him, but I know it wasn't under good circumstances. Probably it was the time he forbade me ever to see Laurie again. I've got to admit it was a weird feeling. Poor guy. He looked like he'd aged twenty years." Adam swallowed. "He treated me badly, but I know how much he loved Laurie—as much as I did. She was all he had."

Everyone was quiet for a minute, and then Adam continued, his voice low. "He looked around kind of nervously for a minute, and then he walked up and looked me straight in the eye. He didn't say anything for a moment, just stared at me. Then he said, his voice kind of wobbling, 'I was wrong about you, son, totally wrong.' And then he shook my hand."

Adam fell quiet, thinking. When he looked up again, his eyes were bright with tears. "It made me feel as if things weren't so bad, that handshake, and I could almost envision going on without Laurie."

Elizabeth felt a lump form in her throat as she listened to Adam's story. She couldn't believe how much she admired him. She just hoped with all her heart that life would be good to him from then on, that he would somehow find things to make up for the pain he'd suffered.

Something told her, given Adam's courage and conviction, that he would.

"What's wrong with you?" Elizabeth demanded, hurrying into the living room and stopping short when she saw the dark scowl on her twin's face. It was the following week, and the

Wakefield household had gradually fallen back into a normal routine. Adam was back at work and seemed to be doing as well as could be expected. He was relying heavily on the Wakefields for support as he began to adjust to the loss he had suffered.

"Nothing. I'm just annoyed that Mr. Robb ran our story under Seth's byline without even mentioning me," Jessica grumbled. "So what did I get out of all that hard work?"

She and Seth had written a wonderful story together, and she knew they had every reason to be proud of their work. "Millionaire's Son Confesses to Hamilton Murder," the headlines had run. Under it, in two full pages of dense text, was the dramatic story of Tom Winslow's unrequited love for Laurie, his bouts of depression, his scheme to frame Adam, and the horrible murder he had committed that awful Tuesday night. Seth had gotten all the credit, and Jessica was fuming, even though part of the article had been devoted to her.

"Well, you've got Seth's appreciation, for one thing," Elizabeth said with a smile. "I can see why Mr. Robb didn't want to run your byline, Jess. After all, you really are just an intern, despite the fact that you're a local hero."

"Well, *I* wrote most of the story," Jessica said. "And I was the one who had to do all the dangerous stuff to get hold of the real truth. I can't believe *he's* come out of this whole thing so well."

"Excuse me," Elizabeth said, opening the letter from Jeffrey she had just picked up on the counter, "but it seems to me that Seth isn't the only one who came out of this looking surprisingly good. I mean, let's face it, Jessica, for somebody who was basically sneaking around and forging letters—"

"I thought we'd dropped that subject," Jessica said, hurt. "I mean, I'm glad for Seth and everything. I really wanted to help his career. But I wish Mr. Robb had given *me* some credit."

Elizabeth plopped down on the couch and began reading Jeffrey's letter. "Maybe next time," she murmured.

Jessica leaned over and picked up the binoculars lying on the couch. "Seth's going to write a mystery about me," she announced, getting up and wandering over to the window. She peered through the binoculars at the Bennets' garden. "I wonder what it'll be about?"

"Jessica, what are you doing?" Elizabeth demanded, putting down the letter and looking at her sister.

"Nothing," Jessica said vaguely, turning the lens to get better focus. "Hey," she said suddenly. "Mrs. Bennet is dragging a crate out from the cellar. I wonder what's inside it?"

"Jess, haven't you learned your lesson? There are enough mysteries around without your having to spy on the neighbors to dredge them up," Elizabeth said sharply.

Jessica didn't looked convinced. "You may be right," she said, in exactly the sort of voice that suggested that she doubted it.

No matter what Elizabeth said, Jessica intended to tell Seth about Mrs. Bennet and the crate. And she was determined to start keeping an eye on some of the other people in the neighborhood, too.

Now that she'd discovered what a knack she had for solving mysteries, Jessica wasn't about to let one happen right under her nose without taking matters into her own hands!